PLAIN OF DARKNESS

PLAIN OF DARKNESS

DAVID LAMBKIN

IVY

IVY PUBLISHING
LONDON • EDINBURGH • SYDNEY
JOHANNESBURG

PLAIN OF DARKNESS

First edition, first impression 1992

Set in 10 on 13 pt Palatino
Printed and bound by Gutenberg Book Printers

ISBN 0 620 16626 6

This book is entirely a work of fiction and the characters bear no relation whatsoever to any person living or dead.

THIS BOOK IS FOR
OLIVE MARY
1908–1989

I

Your whole life now must be one of longing
if you are to receive perfection.

The Cloud of Unknowing.

II

What a woman tells her lover in desire
should be written out on air and running water.

Catullus.

PROLOGUE

You may never have placed the barrel of a four-four magnum revolver in your mouth. If you have, you will know that the result is not dignified; nor is it easy to achieve since you must open wide, bunching the muscles at the angle of your jaw to accommodate the high front sight. The metal of the long barrel is cold on your tongue. It is the moment of contemplation.

You may then sense your thumb, seemingly of its own volition, draw back the hammer. The serrations are sharp and deep on its recurve and you will hear two crisp clicks as the rebates on the hammer engage the trigger sear. Eternity is within your compass.

It is the echo of this double click in your sinuses, and the certain knowledge that the tiniest pressure of your index finger will spray your most esteemed parts all over the ceiling that returns to wake you night after night, and tease you with the bleak promise of eternal peace.

PART ONE

THE SEA

The dragon-green,
the luminous,
the dark,
the serpent-haunted sea.

James Elroy Flecker. The Gates of Damascus.

ONE

I built my house of wood on a narrow tongue of land that struck out from the end of a rocky promontory toward the sea. In the beginning it was a good house full of children's laughter but now it was empty and as cold as a nun's kiss. I loved it still despite the emptiness. When the reality is gone we have the memory yet and for some of us the memory will ever be better than the way it all was.

I was thirty six then and had taken refuge in that house in the teeth of the wind to recuperate from a divorce – my second – and the loss of my adopted daughter and her mother, Eva.

Her absence reproached me constantly. There was a connection I could not fathom between my grief and random events in the natural world: the way the waves broke or the flight of a tern pinned against the storm. Seeing these things, my despair grew; as, earlier in my life, the sight of a baboon troop foraging at nightfall on the edge of the savannah, the wind turning their fur, broke my heart as finally as any woman can.

Loss is strange. I sometimes woke suddenly in the night and felt that I could not remember who I was. I would get up and stand at the big window that overlooked the sea and stare at the constellations as they sank slowly westward into the dark edge of the world. In time I knew from the position of Scorpius exactly how many hours it was till dawn. Orion's swordbelt I knew well, and the Pleiades; and I recalled Sappho's lament: 'The moon is sunk, and the Pleiades and midnight is gone and the hours keep passing and I lie alone ...' But afterwards, when I watched the stars, nothing would occur to me at all and I could even look at the way the wind puckered the water and feel nothing.

In summer the southeast trades whipped across the beach through a gap in the encircling mountains behind the house and hauled the sea out whitecapped as far as the eye could see; but my refuge lay becalmed, sheltered by a chance shoulder of peaks in the mountains above so that at high summer the cottage lay in a still pool of heat. Not all houses on the Atlantic coast are so lucky.

In winter the northwesterly seas brought Atlantic cold and the house and I endured the relentless squalls of June and July. When the winds had been driven day and night by storms out at sea they would bring with them waves that could not be stopped by the steep beach. The wind drove them on into the seagrass in the shallow dunes above and broke them against the seawall before my garden. It seemed the distant storms reached beneath the concrete into the very foundations of the house.

Far out in the bay there was a rock where the waves broke white at high tide. I had scuba'd there on a summer day when the water was still and clear and had seen where the sea had hollowed out the base of the rock into a dark cave. When the tide flowed the waves broke in the cave with a percussive thump that shook the panes in our bedroom windows. My wife and I often lay close together in the night listening to the sound, like distant thunder, as the south Atlantic swells broke there. We also listened to each other's breathing, quietly, even though we each knew the other was awake in the darkness. Now she had gone I lay and listened alone at night and always knew from the sound the sea made whether the tide had changed. Listening to the sea when I woke in the night made the darkness seem less empty, and when the waves thudded in midwinter, the walls of my wooden house shook and I would feel a sudden calmness, although why this should be I cannot understand.

My house is gone now; levelled not by the wind and sea but by a borer beetle who ate away at the wood leaving it light and brittle. The roof collapsed one winter in a cloud of splinters when I was away on holiday; I returned to find a pile of grey driftwood instead of a house. Everything had been looted.

And then there were the dolphins. In summer, schools of bottlenose dolphins came often to my small bay to slide down the face of each breaking wave. Sometimes they played in the warm green shallows like children, watching me with incurious eyes as I looked at them from the rocks. At first I had confused them with sharks. I often saw white-tipped reef sharks swimming in the shallows at dusk, come in close to the beach to hunt; and the curve of the shark's dark fin is mimicked by that of the dolphin.

Their visits were so unexpected and they themselves were so enigmatic, they seemed more than mere dolphins. In time, when I had gained a little wisdom, I came to see them as transfigured gods, come to initiate my wife and me into their mysteries. Once, my adopted child wanted to swim with them, but I said no. The black sickle curve of their fins and their dark bodies made me fearful of them, nor was I a strong swimmer. So we stood there on the rocks hand in hand, the girl and I, and looked at them from the safety of the land. Finally they turned away and disappeared into the deep.

Perhaps I should have let the child swim with them, but at the time I thought she was too young. Perhaps I should have swum with them myself. It's too late now.

There was one companion; my dog of sixteen years, a paunchy black labrador named Ludwig, after the Viennese maestro. He slept at the foot of my bed and woke often at night with a soft whine to tell me of illicitly visiting ghosts in his ageing brain. He had been given to me when I was a young man and had lived with me all that time, moving with me from farm to townhouse, from England to Africa, with grace and unfading loyalty.

The .44 magnum was with me all the time. It was a Ruger Super Blackhawk single-action revolver. Eva had given it to me one birthday because I'd coveted it to protect her and the child. In truth, clumsy and slow, it was not a very good self-defense weapon, but I liked its elegance. It lay beside my bed at night while I slept and in the stillness when sleep failed me I would hold it, the walnut grips smooth in my hands, the long barrel as shiny and cold as a string of black pearls. And on nights when my remorse was at its worst or when memories would not let me be, my eyes would seek out its dark shape where it lay beside my bed, and I would remember the cold barrel on my tongue, the sharp scent of gun oil in my sinus, and the pressure of the trigger beneath my finger.

It was then, towards the end of a long winter, that I met the young girl. She was fourteen and she fell in love with me for eight days. Or so I'd like to think. Like some wicked sprite or a trainee she-devil, she entered my life when all I wanted was to be left alone, disrupted my routines, disturbed my peace and destroyed my autonomy. She also forced me to enter the dark cave of my past. Then she left as quickly and enigmatically as she'd come.

Her name was Mandy.

TWO

I met her one cold day on the winter beach. The day was overcast, the sky darker than the sea. I was walking with Ludwig along the two-mile curve of sand that stretched between my rocky point and the next where there lived a blind old man named Daniel Lockhart who often strode the beach. Today he was nowhere in sight. The wind was down, there was no hint of sun and Ludwig was galloping stiff-necked ahead of me along the beach. Shrieking gulls scattered from untidy piles of kelp when he stalked them and hovered tormentingly just out of reach of his snapping teeth. Just a few years ago he would have caught the unwary.

There was much driftwood above the tideline unloaded by the winter seas and I'd collected an armfull for my big stone fireplace when Ludwig suddenly collapsed in midstride with a soft whimper and rolled onto his side. I put down my wood and knelt beside him. His heart made a sturdy bump against my fingers but the white nictitating membranes had slipped from the inner corner of his eyes across each iris. For the first time I realized how silver with age his muzzle had become. I wondered what to do. If I lost him ... if he died ... no more chasing gulls, no more running on the beach. A vacant crab-shell lay beside him, light as a grass-stalk.

'Is your dog sick?'

I turned. The voice belonged to a girl-child, a teenager in jeans and a red jersey. Twelve? Thirteen? I had not noticed her. She might almost have materialised out of sea-spume and wind.

'I think so. He just fell over,' I answered. I felt Ludwig's pulse. It was fast but regular. The girl knelt beside me. She had unfashionably long hair the colour of polished brass.

'It's a stroke! Labradors have them. I had a Labrador and he did just that. It's serious but not fatal.' She put her hand on his chest to feel his heart. Her hands were small and lovely, tanned to the colour of the highlights in her hair.

'I see.' I stroked Ludwig's silver muzzle. 'I'd better carry him home.'

'You can't carry the dog and the wood. I'll take the wood. Why do you call him Ludwig?'

'After Beethoven.'

'Why Beethoven?' She wrinkled up her nose. I bent and picked up Ludwig.

'I like Beethoven.'

'Why? I don't. I like heavy metal rock. Mummy likes Beethoven.'

'Does she? Do you think you could poke his paw back through there? Thanks'.

Her hands were deft and gentle.

'Why on earth do you like Beethoven?' she asked again, struggling with the pieces of driftwood. We trudged back together along the beach through the dry powder sand. She was beside me, the driftwood in her arms. Her eyes were dark blue. I could feel Ludwig's heartbeat against my chest.

'Beethoven? I enjoy his music because he's not like Mozart. Do you know Mozart? Mozart was a sort of god. And a child. You can't learn from a god how to live as a mortal, or from a child. So I like Beethoven.'

'You look a bit like a god,' she said unselfconciously.

I glanced at her sharply, but she wasn't smiling.

'No, really. I've often seen you running along the beach and swimming,' she said. 'One of those ancient gods. You look like that statue -Poseidon? I've seen a photograph. My mother likes it. He was Greek,' she added helpfully, 'except your nose looks a bit like a potato.'

'I don't have a beard. And why haven't I seen you?'

She smiled. 'You look like him, even without a beard. And I'm always in the water. Invisible . . .'

'That's because he was getting old like me but kept in shape going to gym every day.'

'Why do you go to gym every day? You don't seem like one of those silly muscle-men who normally go. Mummy had a boyfriend like that once, he spent ages combing his hair in the mirror and watching himself in shop windows.'

I decided not to ask why mummy had boyfriends and said, 'I dive quite a lot and you need to be fit to dive in the water here, it's quite treacherous.'

This answer seemed to satisfy her and she said, 'My mother goes to gym every day, too.'

'Is that so?'

'She says you have to fight age.'

'Does she indeed? She must be an energetic woman. How old is she?'

'Thirty four. How old are you?'

'Thirty six. This is my house. And you? How old are you?'

'I know. All the children know your house, you're famous.'

'Why?' I asked, intrigued.

'They say your house is full of skulls.'

'I've got some skulls. I like them.'

'So do I. And I'm fourteen. Well, thirteen and three-quarters, really.'

'Open the gate, would you? And the front door. You'll find the key under that glass buoy. You can put the wood under the eave.'

She packed the driftwood neatly on top of the existing pile, found the key under the buoy and unlocked the door. Inside, she marvelled politely at my collection of skulls, supervised the bedding-down of Ludwig in his basket, gave me precise advice on his care and feeding and left with an unsolicited promise to check on his progress the next day. I watched her as she walked off down the beach. The rising wind was lifting her hair. At that distance she looked like a woman. When I closed my front door and turned to look at my sitting room, it was emptier than ever.

I phoned the vet. He came, gave Ludwig an injection, left some pills and looked grave. It was clear from his prognosis that Ludwig would take some time to recover. Work was slow at the moment in my world of advertising photography so I phoned my secretary and told her I would to be away for a few days, looking after Ludwig. She was sympathetic. She'd phone if there was an emergency. Ludwig slept peacefully in his basket. I missed his little sleeping whines and as I cooked dinner and set my table, I kept going back to look at him. He seemed to be in no pain, but who can tell?

It struck me that evening as I settled down in my big armchair with a double tot of after dinner Laphroaig and "The Cloud of Unknowing" that the child – I still didn't know her name – was the first person other than Daniel Lockhart to cross my threshold in nearly five months. I was not sure what that meant. But the years that had passed since my wife left had brought with them no cessation of loss, no filling of the void, no end to the self-recrimination and lacerations, none of the subtle healing and mending and suturing of wounds for which time is so unjustly famous. Truly, time is no healer. The patient is no longer there.

THREE

I woke before dawn and went to see Ludwig. He seemed weak but was pleased to see me and he drank a little warm milk. Gazing without delight at myself in the bathroom mirror I decided to break the rule of a lifetime and let my beard grow. I went outside. It was still dark and the sea was flat and the skyline rancid with the effusions of the small industries on the far side of Table Bay.

I stood on the porch and sipped my coffee and watched the kelp gulls glide in to the beach from their morning forays. I felt uneasy but could not say why. It was not Ludwig; was it the child? Sifting through memory I found the reason: in one of my bedroom cupboards was a suitcase filled with clothes that my ex-wife had elected to leave behind. They were clothes I had loved to watch her wear in our private erotic rituals, and I think she'd left them as an act of kindness. Or perhaps cruelty. I had found it impossible to throw away this Pandora's box with its talismans of our past; but, I told myself, the clothes meant little enough. They were simply there to be endured and discarded.

I found the case in the bedroom cupboard, placed it on the bed and opened it. There was a hint of Ma Griffe, Eva's perfume, on the silk and satin garments, but I was beyond the reach of perfume.

'Hallo? Are you there?' called a voice from outside. The child.

'Yes. Coming ...' Through the big glass doors I could see her silhouetted against the light from the sea, the early glitter outlining her young legs through her summer frock. I opened the door.

'Hello,' she said. Bright eyes, hair still damp, shampoo scent all about her, lips open. 'You're letting your beard grow!'

'Hello yourself. I don't know your name.'

'Mandy Thetiss. What's yours? Your beard looks good. I brought your dog some liver.'

'That's kind. Thetiss? Greek? I'm Paul.'

'Hello Paul. Yes, my father, not mummy. Well, ask me in ...'

I stood aside. The frock was faded blue cotton exactly the colour of the cornflowers in my grandmother's garden in England.

'Where's Ludwig?'

'In his basket in the pantry.'

'How is he?'

She led the way to the pantry.

'Not at all bad. I sat with him for an hour earlier.'

'Is he taking his medicine? Did the vet come?'

'Yes, he came and yes he's taking his pills. He says he's quite old and I've got to feed him a special diet. Chicken, plenty of vegetables, lots of fluids for his kidneys, not too much red meat.'

Ludwig wagged his tail and licked Mandy's face as she cuddled him. He tried to get up but couldn't. I turned away.

'Is liver red meat?' she asked.

'Yes.'

'He can't eat the liver then. Have you had breakfast?'

'No.'

'Good. We'll have the liver. I'll lay the table on your porch,' she said. 'Is that alright?'

'Of course.'

She bustled around finding cutlery, a tablecloth and even the clips I use to hold down the cloth in summer. I smelt bacon and liver cooking. She hummed tunelessly. I found her bossiness rather endearing; people who live alone like to have their strict routines disturbed. I fed Ludwig shredded chicken by hand and watched him eat. His eyes were dull and I hoped he was in no pain. He ate very little chicken but wagged his tail when I stroked him.

'Breakfast,' called Mandy from the porch. I went out. She was sitting at the table and had dished scrambled eggs, bacon and very rare liver. She poured tomato sauce onto her scrambled eggs, creating a mess that bore an uncanny resemblance to blood and pus.

'Mummy won't let me do that at home,' she confided.

'I can see why.'

'Do you like liver?' she asked through a mouthful.

'Yes,' I lied. 'Don't talk with your mouth full.'

'You sound like Mummy. I love liver, but some people don't at all. I like the taste of the blood.'

'Really?'

'Oh yes. Sometimes I don't even cook it, I just eat it raw. Mummy says its barbaric.'

'Have you eaten steak tartare?'

'No. What's that?'

'Raw minced steak with seasoning.'

'That sounds great. Is it bloody?'

'It's raw,' I said, wondering if she had little pointed teeth.

'Where do you get it? Restaurants?'

'Yes. Actually I make it . . .'

'Do you? Will you make me some? Very bloody?'

'Yes.'

'When?'

I was appalled to hear myself say, 'It's very early for you to decide, I know, but if you like I'll make some for you for lunch; that is, if you want to come back later. If you haven't got anything to do . . .'

'Thanks, that's nice. I'm not going home for lunch, I told Mummy already, she's got her father coming for lunch and when he's there she doesn't even notice anyone else. He thinks he's so important because he's got some kind of big business. He's Mummy's hero. I think she loves him a bit too much, actually. She's got a photograph of him next to her bed and a painting of him on the wall in the sitting room that he gave her, with a candle on the table and a basket full of fruit. It looks like a church. Ugh.'

'I know a woman like that. Awful.'

'Awful. He's awful. So are all his friends. One of them offered me fifty rand if I took off my top and showed him my tits,' she said casually.

'What? Good God.'

'He's awful, he smells of brandy and he hugs all my friends too long. He's really stupid.'

'Who? The father?'

'No, silly, the friend.'

'And did you?'

'Did I what?'

'Take the fifty rand,' I said primly.

'Don't be stupid. I told you, I don't like him. He smells. You don't smell. At least, you do, but it's nice. Lemons.'

'I like the smell.'

'Lemons. Mummy always smells lovely, she smells of Ma Griffe. Do you know what that means? I put some on today for you, smell . . .'

She stretched out her arm with her wrist offered to me. There were small blue veins beneath her skin. Would she ever be tempted to breach them for love, I wondered.

'Yes,' I said. 'I know what it means.'

'Do you like it?'

'I've always liked it,' I said and watched a trickle of liver blood run down her chin. She licked it up with a tongue as deft as a cat's. I wondered if this untamed child spent her days asleep in a coffin to emerge at dusk and fly the skies looking for blood.

'Where are you at school?' I asked.

'St. Michael's.'

'Boarder? Day girl?'

'Weekly boarder. I love school. I love the dorm. All the girls in my dorm are super. We're on holiday now. And you? What work do you do?'

'I'm a photographer.'

'Really? I've never met a photographer before. What do you take photographs of?'

'I used to do a lot of fashion but now I do mostly advertising.'

'Do you take photographs of naked ladies?' she asked with a naughty grin.

'Not any more.'

'Will you take photographs of me?'

'Perhaps one day.'

'Why not now?'

'Not in the mood.'

'I'd like to be a model and go to exciting places and earn lots of money,' she said dreamily.

'Modelling's boring. So are models.'

'Are they? How do you know?'

'My first wife was a model.'

'Was she boring?'

'Very.'

'Is that why you're divorced?'

'We didn't have a lot in common.'

'Do you have a lot of girlfriends?'

'Not any more.'

'But when you were young?'

'Am I too old for girlfriends now?'

'Never, you're just right. No, I mean you know about perfume and stuff and I feel at home with you and I know you like me and I think you like women too, not just girls. You're not like granpa's friends at all.'

I stared at her.

'Well?' she persisted.

'Well yes. I have had quite a lot of girlfriends. And wives.'

'How many?'

'Two wives.'

'And girlfriends?'

'Enough.'

'Ten? Twenty? Thirty?'

'It's rude to count.'

'Forty? Fifty?' She stared at me. I said nothing.

'If I was a woman, I'd like you,' she said thoughtfully. 'I think you're gentle and I'd like to see you cry.'

'Thanks for breakfast,' I said quickly to change the subject.

'Pleasure. It was wonderful. I love breakfast best of all.'

'Tea? Coffee? Hot chocolate?'

'No, thanks. Oh, look,' she said, pointing out to sea. 'Dolphins. See? They came ...'

Far out where the slight southeaster was flecking the sea beyond the shelter of the bay there was a faint widening vee with a telltale flurry of white at its apex.

'They're early this year,' I said, watching.

'Yes, I called them to come,' she said. 'To help Ludwig.' I looked at her.

'Don't you believe me?'

'It's not that. It just sounded strange.'

'Do you like dolphins?'

'What do you think?'

'Yes, I know you do. You understand. No-one else does. They all live in such little worlds. I've swum with the dolphins often. Have you?''

'No, not yet.'

'You should, you'd love it. That's how I can call them, you see. They're my friends. I call them with a big old conch shell.' She stood up from the table, folding her napkin neatly. 'Come on, I want to see the rest of your house.'

I walked with her slowly through the cottage. She liked, I thought, all the right things, things I had collected over years that held no meaning for anybody else. The two whale jawbones I'd found washed up one winter that now stood silent and white in the corner of the sitting room: many people who saw them said they looked tawdry and worm-eaten. I didn't think so and it seemed Mandy agreed, because she stroked one and said softly, 'He must have been so big and so beautiful.' And my baboon skull, picked up all those years ago on the Plain of Darkness when we went looking for the old bull elephant wounded by poachers: rain-bleached and vacant-socketed, it discomfited many people, but not Mandy. She touched the long fighting teeth, traced their deep roots, questioned me closely about baboons, their society and habits, their diet and family life, but not once did she ask me why I kept the skull. She knew. She stared at the long hundred pound elephant tusk that was propped in one corner and said, 'Where did you get that?' And when I replied, 'We shot the elephant,' she didn't erupt into a diatribe against hunting. She simply said, 'I know you didn't kill him for no reason . . .' She turned to me, her eyes inscrutable, and said, 'Will you show me your guns?'

'What makes you so sure I've got guns?' I said.

'I just know,' she murmured. 'Please?'

I opened the gunsafe and took out the rifles and shotguns I'd inherited from my grandfather and showed them to her. She stroked the wood of the twelve bore William Evans shotgun that glowed with life like a violin and ran her fingers over the twin hammers, recurved like those of a highway-man's pistol.

She was full of questions. 'Why did your grandfather have all these guns?'

'He came to Africa as a young man; and before he went back to England to marry my grandmother he made a lot of money shooting buffalo for rations for the plantation workers in Portuguese East Africa. He was a bit of an adventurer. And he used this one –' – I indicated the Jeffrey .450 No.2 double barrel Express rifle – '– for hunting elephant for their ivory in the rainy season . . .' She tried to pick up the rifle and failed.

'Ooof! That's heavy. Can you shoot it?'

'My grandfather taught me when I was young. He spent hours drawing elephant skulls and showing me where to aim for a brainshot.'

'Why?'

'My grandmother told him to.'

'Why?'

'She was a gypsey, she had a sort of second sight; she could predict things. Witchy . . .'

'Golly.'

'Yes. Odd she thought I'd need to know how to shoot an elephant, though.'

She peered into the safe and found the four-four Magnum.

'What's that?' she asked in a quiet voice.

'My revolver.'

I took it out, emptied the cylinder and handed it to her. She took it reluctantly, staring at the long, cold barrel. She handed it back to me. 'I don't like that. Why did you get it?'

'Eva gave it to me. My wife. Ex-wife.'

She shook her head. 'I don't like it, and I don't think you should have it.' She turned away.

I locked away the guns and she moved on to look at the floor-to-ceiling bookshelves in the study;examined the books closely – ('Have you read all these? Golly.') – demanded an explanation of the wordprocessor, and when she noticed my two aqualungs, became thoroughly animated.

'Hey, I forgot! You told me you scuba.'

'When?'

'On the beach. I do too. I got my NAUI card last year.'

She then riffled through my filing cabinet, looked thought-fully but without comment at a salacious photograph she found there of an old girlfriend in a lacy corset and stockings, but when we came to the bedroom she stopped dead when she saw the reproduction Bosch above my double bed.

She stared at it then said in a soft voice, 'I've seen that before.'

'Oh? Where?'

'I don't know ...' She walked closer and stared at it. 'They're all naked ...'

'It's called "The Garden of Earthly Delights,"' I said.

'Yes, I know ...' She watched it for some time in silence, then turned to the open suitcase on the bed. I felt momentarily embarrassed.

'Whose clothes are these?'

'My wife's.'

'Is she staying here?'

'No. I'm going to throw them away.'

'Why?' she asked, picking up a soft dark blue silk skirt. 'This is beautiful ...'

'They remind me too much of her.'

'They're beautiful.'

'Yes,' I said drily, 'Eva certainly knew how to buy clothes.' She eagerly examined the contents of the case. Slingback shoes, satin blouses, slips, lace teddies, brand new silk panties, suspender belts, skirts.

I watched her. She made me uneasy: there was something in her eyes of the sexual arrogance I always saw in Eva. When Eva first revealed to me her erotic obsession with dressing up like a very expensive hooker I wondered if she hoped to satisfy me with a sexual persona and keep her real self inviolate behind all that satin and lace. I never found out.

Mandy held up a black satin g-string, looked at me with knowing eyes and said with a little smile, 'These are really naughty. Mummy wears them sometimes.'

I shrugged. She stroked a gunmetal silk blouse.

'Please can I try some of them on?' She looked up at me. Her eyes were dark blue, all pupil, almost black.

'They won't fit you,' I said.

'Yes they will,' she said, examining a label. 'Your wife's about Mummy's size and I can wear quite a lot of her clothes. I'm bigger than I look. Please?'

'Of course,' I said, and turned to leave.

'Don't go,' she said. 'I've got a swimming costume on.' She unbuttoned her frock and shrugged it off and it fell and lay in a pale blue pool at her feet.

★

When Mandy left me after lunch it was nearly four o' clock and a storm was coming fast from the north-west. A line of dark cloud sulked on the horizon and thunder burped and farted but there was no telltale flicker of lightning to chase the strings of hunting cormorants back to their roosts. I tapped the barometer and the needle dropped back. It was going to be a bad storm.

I cleared plates, stacked them in the dishwasher, switched it on and returned to the porch with a soft and ancient woollen jersey and a Bombay gin and tonic to watch the weather coming in, and to think about what had happened with the girl.

She'd consumed the steak tartare with the passion of a starving hyena, making little noises of pleasure and drinking a glass of wine-and-soda: 'I promise I love your steak tartare even more than strawberry ripple, more than raw liver. Promise you'll make it again. Promise.' I promised. But all through the meal I'd been able to see nothing but her body in the tight black one-piece costume as she dressed herself in my wife's clothes in the bedroom.

And I felt a tremor of fear. I needed detachment in order to liberate my heart from its affections and leave myself free to contemplate my trivial place in the unfolding universe. But this child had eluded my watchmen. She had entered my life without my permission.

It was not simply her beauty, nor the grace of her; it was that combination of beauty of form and apparent lack of artifice that worked so powerfully to entrance. But there was something darker too, something reptilian, a shiver from the brainstem. She was jailbait, and there was a potent sexual tension in the bedroom as she stripped to her costume and began to dress. I was fascinated: she was quite aware of the effect she was having but pretended innocence.

As she began to dress – skirt, blouse, shoes – she had all the coquette's moves: the quick encompassing glance and half-turn in front of the looking glass to check the seat of the skirt, flirting with her hair as she piled it up into a rough chignon, the curve of waist into buttock into thigh when she raised her foot to slip on one of the slingbacks. A little girl dressing up in mummy's clothes. But dressed, she was no child. She was a woman. And she'd learnt none of it; she was born knowing.

19

And she was Eva before Eva knew me; she was everything I did not know about Eva: her youth, her growing soul, her sweet tentative sexuality.

At the end of it all when she was demure again in her blue frock, she sat beside me on the bed and took my hand and said: 'Did you like that?'

I said nothing.

She smiled slightly and said, 'I know you did.'

'Do you?'

'Yes. Did I remind you of your wife?'

I watched her and said nothing.

'Do you miss her a lot?'

'Sometimes.'

'And do you think I looked pretty?'

'Yes. Very.'

'But did you really really enjoy it?'

'Yes.'

She nodded and stared at me with eyes the colour of Curacao Blue. 'Would you like me to come and dress for you again one day, be your wife for you again?'

I closed my eyes and hoped Lockhart would forgive me. 'Yes,' I said.

'Tomorrow?'

I shrugged.

'Good. I'll come early, then we can do it for a long time,' she said in a soft contented voice. 'But you'll have to keep the clothes, then, won't you?'

'Yes, I will,' I said.

'Good.' She carefully folded all the clothes and packed them neatly back into the suitcase but paused just as she was about to close the lid. 'I can smell a perfume on these,' she said. 'What is it?'

'I think you already know,' I said.

She smiled at me and nodded and closed the case.

When it grew too cold on the porch I went inside and restlessly stalked the cottage before going to the bedroom to stare at the places she'd been.

She'd stood there and there, had pirouetted there, had sat on the bed there. And I'd watched her there, seen her mulberry nipples pressed against the thin Speedo, longed to

20

touch the taut swell of her pudendum, bellied and split like a ripe fig in summer heat. What was happening to me? I was appalled that the lust had been so instant. And so pointless! Once gratified, it would be gone and we'd lie there unable to think of anything to say to one other.

And we were so different. Yes, I'd had lovers who were empty headed and trivial; but I thought I'd learnt how to avoid that particular travail. I needed to fuel my damnation and salvation with the wisdom and folly of those who'd gone before me, but Mandy needed none of that. She already knew everything she needed to know. She'd been born with knowledge.

Beside my bed there was a copy of Petrarch's sonnets to Laura. I'd been trying to read the Italian with the aid of a parallel English text. I picked it up, opened it at random and read: '... broken by the years and by the tired road ...' What sense could that ever make to Mandy? She would never tire. One day she would simply cease to be. But despite this upsurge of lust that diminished and demeaned me, I wanted to suck the juice from her, feel her clitoris on the tip of my tongue as firm and fleshed as a ripe pomegranate seed.

As penance for these fantasies I stood in front of my full-length mirror and took off all my clothes and stared at myself. The signs of middle aged decay were clearly there in the slight softness at my waist that no amount of situps on the incline board could banish, in the knobbly knee where intrepid surgeons had carved out rugby-damaged cartilage and carelessly resealed my skin, in the sad cluster of chicken neck and giblets that skulked in a thicket of black pubic hair. The look in my eyes that of an ourang-outang too long in the zoo. My body was fighting a losing war against time: connective tissue was stiffening, muscles were losing their snap. I knew there were still hints in the way I moved of the athlete I'd once been, long ago, but time would soon remove those too. There's nothing so silly as an old sportsman bewailing his lost prowess.

Thinking of Mandy, I felt so old. Not that I cared about the loss of youth, I was too far past vanity for that. But what about this child? Had it come to this? Rejected by my woman, was I now fit only to impress little girls with my erudition and charm? Was I about to become a sweaty paedophile who surreptitiously fondled nubile girls while pretending to play hide-and-seek or rounders? Had my contact with women soured me into this laughable clown? Surely I was not going to betray myself? No, I told myself. You won't.

But despite my moral posturings, I carefully unpacked all of Eva's clothes and hung them in her empty cupboard in my bedroom. My first betrayal. What would the austere Daniel Lockhart say about that?

FOUR

At first I could not see why Daniel Lockhart had entered my life; understanding only came later. True, he was a constant quiet admonishment: he lived a life of spartan bachelorhood. In his house there was no unnecessary luxury, in his demeanour no sign of metaphysical ecstasy. And yet I was convinced he had confronted evil and not flinched; he had found some arcane knowledge that comforted. I envied him.

Clearly, his faith had been hard-won and made either easier or harder by the fact that he was blind. On his blindness he himself had nothing to say. He was absolutely without self-pity and simply ignored his affliction. There were rumours: some said he'd been a real hellraiser when young, a sailor, and had lost his sight in a barroom brawl in Djakarta at the hands of a Lascar seaman with a broken bottle; others, less generously, that he'd been shot by a jealous husband. When I questioned him, he simply shook his head and laughed. He referred only once to his blindness in my presence, when he remarked casually that 'some people must be blind before they can see.' At the time, I thought of Milton and James Joyce; but when I mentioned them he simply smiled. Now I understand why.

His blindness was no handicap. Each day I would scan the sea and beach with my binoculars, searching for something; for what I was never quite certain. And since Lockhart was a great fisherman I would often see him walking alone along the beach with his cane casting rod and white stick, the collar of his dark blue reefer jacket turned up against the wind, surrounded by screaming gulls who flocked to him to be fed from his bait-box.

We met first on a winter day when I was standing on the rocks at the sea's end of the promontory, watching the big waves beat at the old oil-tanker wrecked there. One night while under tow to the knacker's yard in Hong Kong she'd broken her lines in a sudden squall and run aground bow-first on the far headland. The sea had hammered in her plates on the windward side that winter and when the waves marched in across the Atlantic and burst inside the hull, a great plume of spray issued tall and white from the rusted funnel and fell back like rain into the withdrawing waves.

Lockhart had walked silently up behind me as I stood watching and the first knowledge I had of his presence was the light tap of his stick on my ankle. I turned in surprise and saw a tall stooped man of about sixty, with a nose hooked like the beak of a bird of prey, wearing a pair of black-glassed spectacles that did not quite conceal the moulding of scar tissue that extended from temple to temple. His thick hair, now silver, had once been dark. He wore an old Burberry and a crew-necked sweater, and I could see from the breadth of shoulder that he must have been very powerful when young.

'I'm so sorry if I startled you,' he said.

'Not at all,' I replied. 'Ought you to be out on the rocks?'

'I know them quite well,' he said. 'You're watching the wreck?'

'Yes.'

'It must be quite a sight.'

'You live at the far end of the bay, don't you?' I asked.

'Yes, and you at the other,' he replied. 'My goodness it's chilly.'

' I can offer you tea, if you have the time.'

'On a day like this, I think a little scotch is called for,' he said with a smile.

'Laphroaig?'

'None better.'

He was very wary. It took some months of casual friendship before he trusted me; but then he began to drop in whenever he felt like it and we often fished together in comfortable silence, in winter celebrating each other's catches and losses with draughts of Laphroaig from my hip flask, in summer drinking a thin dry white wine he doted on.

24

One afternoon, when the elf run was on and we'd each caught a half-dozen of the hard-fighting silver-green fish, he invited me to his cottage for a celebratory drink.

The cottage was very bare; he had no use now for paintings or books. But peering inquisitively through a doorway I could see on a table beside his bed two silver framed photographs of a dark-haired woman. This struck me as strange until I remembered that I once saw through my binoculars an old dark blue car that looked like a Bentley draw up at dusk on the shale drive outside his cottage.

Intrigued, I kept watching; and saw a dark-haired woman wearing a long black evening dress emerge from the car and knock at his door. I saw the door open and she disappeared inside. I could not tell her age. This piqued my interest and I spied on him shamelessly until I discerned a pattern: the dark-haired woman called on him once a month, always at dusk, always in evening dress, and stayed till after midnight. I never asked him about her. Who could?

Although his sitting room was very bare, Lockhart had obviously at one time indulged expensive tastes. His floor was covered with worn old Persians and his wine rack was full of wines from Medoc I'd heard of but never tasted. He insisted he prefered Old Brown Sherry.

But I was more interested in his large copy of the eleventh century Chola bronze of the god Shiva, dancing the cosmic dance of creation. When I questioned Lockhart he answered reluctantly, saying he didn't like to talk about it. But I pressed him, wondering if he was a Hindu. He was silent for a time, then said: 'This is Shiva the Destroyer in his manifestation as Nataraja, the many-armed God of the Dance. Shiva has many personalities: sometimes he is one who is alone, one who withdraws and is untamed.'

'And?'

He sighed. 'You don't give up, do you?'

'No. And?'

'See the circle of flames?'

'Yes?'

'That's the prabhamandala, a kind of divine fire, the rhythm of the universe. If you look, you'll see that it grows out of a lotos flower.'

'That's significant?'

'The lotos is the Hindu symbol of enlightenment. You know nothing about this?'

'Nothing.'

'Very well. See that dwarfish child the god's dancing on? That's Apasma-rapurusa, the symbol of human ignorance. The left hand at the back holds Damaru, the fire of destruction. And there you have it. Creation and destruction, all in one.'

'Why four arms?'

'I'm not sure. They each have a meaning. The front arm is in the position that says to the viewer: Do not be afraid.'

'Do not be afraid?'

'Yes. Do not be afraid. Do you like it?'

'Very much,' I said slowly. 'Very much indeed . . .'

He became my self-appointed spiritual advisor. He gave me a fine copy of the Cloud of Unknowing, recited to me the Bhagavad Gita, and censured me gently for my lack of vocation. And sometimes he would visit me to drink a good malt whisky and coax me to accept his view as the only one tenable by a man of intelligence who loved the universe with his whole being, not merely his intellect. And when I confessed my inability to understand what the unmoved mover willed for me, he chided me for my lack of faith and told me to trust my instincts.

'You've been taught too well,' he said. 'They've trained you not to trust your intuition. Ignore them; no one can teach you; but you must know this: what you are looking for is already inside you. Remember what Herakleitos said?'

'No?'

'"Although knowledge of the logos is common to all, most men act as if they had insight of their own."' To discover your own knowledge of the logos you must learn to wait, he said, for the stillness to come upon you, learn to wait for the stillness of God.

Still, tonight I could not read, could not settle, and the stillness of God was noticeably absent. The wind hustled reassuringly about the house, the trees creaked and Ludwig twitched; but my mind was not on epiphanies nor spiritual perfection but was beset by visions of the child's sweet rump as it clenched and relaxed inside my wife's skirts. I was prey to thoughts of enveloping flesh and shocked to discover they were elicited by the body of a fourteen year old girl. The hair on her arms and legs had been as pale and soft as peach fur. I wondered how she would taste; I could taste her already. Before I slept I opened the blinds and looked at the sky. Thunderclouds were stalking the moon.

In sleep a dream came and woke me. Mandy was standing in a dark empty place and her body was coldly luminous. She beckoned me and I followed her down a dark passage but then the solid ground gave way beneath me and I fell into emptiness and then I woke. I chased the shadow of the dream down a narrowing corridor of memory but it lost me in the dark and I lay awake for a long time listening, then got up from the bed and opened the blinds and looked out. Why was this strange child calling up dreams?

The sea was a rustling black taffeta dress, the sky spindrift cloud, waiting for rain. A tiny brainspurt of chemicals produced Eva. My love, my wife. Swimming deep in the pool of your new lover's breathing, will you ever think of me? When he kisses you, will his mouth heal the wounds I made? Futile night questions.

The stars said nothing and below the surface of the glittering sea small luminous creatures squeezed themselves into crevices in the rocks when a tremor in the water betrayed the presence of a killer fish. I felt for the cold metal of the .44 magnum Ruger beside the bed and went to sleep with its butt in my hand.

That night the storm broke. I woke to hear the windows rattling in their frames. A gale growled somewhere out at sea. Waves thudded against Cannon Rock out in the bay and the whole air was alive with wind, a portent of eternal darkness. There came a tremble of distant thunder and a whiplash of lighting, gone in an instant. Then the rain began to fall but there was no one beside me in the darkness, frightened by the storm, that I could turn to and hold and comfort through the night.

I woke with the sunrise. The sky was polished silver by wind. Small waves swirled and wrestled with the rocks of my promontory as if trying to reclaim the whole continent. A rosary of dawn cormorants swept past, rising and falling above the groundswell, hunting for food. Gulls foraged in the kelp and seagrass strewn above the tideline. While I watched they found a dead crab, a tiny crayfish, a stiffening fish.

There was a corona of dawn light around the gulls and it seemed as if their bodies could not contain the life that filled them. My wife was like that. She was like a prism; she bent light about her so that the world was different when she had passed. I missed her badly today because her shade had visited me in the night. I resented that: I had buried my dead, my mourning was done, she should leave me be. But I knew that my night visitor had been a creation of my psyche, conjured somehow by the child ...

But I missed her more profoundly than it is possible to miss another human being. I missed her the way a drunk misses his meths, a deadhead his methadone. This is not unusual, I know. But the loss went deeper than flesh; it grated on bone, corrupted my marrow. In the still post-midnight hours when hobgoblins stalk your soul I came to understand that we'd never seen each other as people.

I sometimes felt I'd been bewitched, driven by witches' simples to bond with a creature who looked like a woman but was actually a creation of my underworld. And although my intellect told me this was false I could not escape the feeling that we were chained to each other by powers that were impersonal, were beyond my control, and inhabited a region deeper than I could reach without deranging my mind. I realised only later that, like god and the devil, we had each created the other. I then began to forgive myself. But this is premature.

FIVE

The telephone rang at eight, and an unknown voice said: 'Mr Morgan? My name is Thetiss, Barbara Thetiss. I'm Mandy's mother.'

It was a measure of my guilt that I felt a moment of panic. 'Yes?'

'I'm sorry to bother you so early but Mandy tells me she's going to scuba with you today, and I wanted to make certain.'

Scuba? Naughty little girl . . . 'Certain of what?' I asked carefully.

'You see,' the voice said hesitantly, 'Mandy's a little wild sometimes –'

'I understand. It's her age; I had a teenage daughter too. They're monsters.'

'A fellow sufferer! I hope you'll forgive me, then. I'm not prying . . .'

'We did plan to have a little dive,' I lied. Her relief was plain. 'Oh, I'm so pleased. She loves her diving so and she hasn't got a regular partner. What she calls a "buddy."'

'Please don't worry, Mrs Thetiss,' I said, making a mental note to disembowel Mandy and feed her to the sharks. 'She'll be quite safe. I taught scuba for a while.'

'So kind of you, Mr Morgan.'

'Not at all.'

'And I do hope your dog gets better, Mandy's terribly worried.'

'That's kind of you.'

She had a slightly throaty voice. Gin? Cigarettes?

That morning Mandy came early, dressed in a skirt and jersey, weighed down under her dive-bag, bearing a dish of cooked chicken for Ludwig and a branch of pink blossom for me.

'I stole it on the way,' she confided. 'Do you think that's bad?'

'No. It's very early blossom, isn't it?' She shrugged and put the blossom in a jam-jar of water.

'I'll tell you what is bad, you little monster,' I continued as she looked around for the correct location for my blossom.

'What?'

'Telling lies to your mother.'

'Oh, that,' she said indifferently, but I could tell she was embarrassed. 'I couldn't tell her I was coming to see you just because I like you, she wouldn't understand at all. She'd think awful things. Anyway, I want us to dive together, and I'll dress up for you afterwards too.'

I opened my mouth to speak but she turned to me and said: 'I thought we could dive on the old tanker. It's low tide at nine and very clear after the storm, and I've never dived on it and I bet you have. I want you to show me everything.'

'Where's your aqualung?'

'Empty. But you've got two, I saw.' She glanced at her watch. 'It's only eight now. We've got a bit of time before low tide. Can I see Ludwig?'

She seemed satisfied with Ludwig's progress which tallied with that of her own Labrador who had survived his stroke with only a partially paralysed face which she said gave him a silly lopsided grin like her headmistress. I offered coffee, she chose hot chocolate and sat cross-legged on the floor beside Ludwig, stroking him softly and sipping from her mug. He was strong enough to wag his tail politely. We chatted. It seemed her Mummy with the silken voice had acquired their big house in the divorce settlement.

'The problem is,' she said, 'that even now they're divorced, Mummy still isn't happy. She was unhappy then and she's unhappy now.'

'Perhaps she misses him.'

'No, never. She hates him. She told me so. No, it's not that. You see, she doesn't work. I think she should. She broods. She stares at the sea all day and drinks gin.'

'So do I.'

'Do you?' She picked up one of my sea shells and looked at it.

'This is beautiful. What is it?'

'A scorpion shell.'

'Really? Do they sting when they're alive?'

'No. They just look as if they do.'

'Right! No, I think she needs a boyfriend.'

'Oh yes? Do you have a boyfriend?'

'Not really. I used to have, but Mummy found out and got very cross. So now I have Poseidon instead.'

'Poseidon?'

She smiled. 'I told you. The god of the sea. Mummy's got a picture of him in a book. It folds out really big. You know the one I mean? The one who looks like you?'

I nodded.

'So you understand. He's got no clothes on. He looks so strong but calm. When I want a boyfriend I look at the picture and then I feel good. Do you understand?'

'Yes.'

'It's very private; I told my best friend at school and now she does it too. I showed her how.'

She walked over to my floor-to-ceiling bookshelf and picked up the framed photograph of my ex-wife and her daughter and stared at it. 'She's very beautiful.'

'Yes.'

'What was her name?'

'Eva.'

'No, her whole name.'

'Eva Diana Coletrane.'

'And how old was your daughter?'

'Fourteen.'

'Why did you get divorced?'

'No one big reason.'

She nodded, staring at the picture.

'She's very pretty. Both of them.'

'She was. They were.'

'Were? Are they dead?'

'No. Only for me.'

She smiled at that.

'Do you love them still?'

'Love? Love?'

'You shouldn't have let her go.' she said.

'No.'

'Why did you?'

'We slept differently,' I said uneasily. 'Her bedroom was like a tomb. Airless. Dark. Like the burrow of a hibernating animal. Like Pluto's bedroom.'

'Pluto? The dog?' she said, screwing up her nose in distaste. 'She had a bedroom like a dog kennel? Pouf!'

I stared at her. Her knowledge of mythology evidently extended no further than Poseidon.

'No, not the dog, the jackal. Pluto was the Roman god of the Underworld; the Egyptians had one too, called Anubis; he had the head of a jackal and the body of a man.'

'Golly.' She replaced the photograph. 'Anyway, your house is a bit like a tomb, too, with all these skulls. I like them, but they're a bit eerie. What was her first husband like?'

'I've no idea. She never spoke about him. I gather it was pretty awful, but who knows?' I remembered what Eva had once said about her first husband: 'He murdered a part of my heart.' Was it true? I was no longer sure.

I carried the empty cups to the kitchen. Mandy followed. She opened cupboards and looked in.

'You've got lots of herbs. Do you like cooking?'

'I love it. It's therapeutic.'

'Therapeutic?'

'Makes me feel better.'

'Mummy hates cooking. She drinks gin.'

'That's because she has to cook,' I said.'Come on, let's go, or we'll miss the tide.'

'No, she doesn't,' she said, picking up her dive bag. 'We've got loads of servants; she cooks because she wants to hate something . . .'

SIX

We carried the dive bags and aqualungs two miles along the beach. I found myself a little bemused by my new friend. She'd evidently adopted me, and it amused me that she'd not consulted me at all; she'd simply assumed the role of 'best friend.' I liked her grit: she trudged doggedly on under the weight of her dive bag and aqualung, a small trace of sweat on her upper lip.

When we reached the end of the beach we struggled our equipment up onto the cluster of rocks where the old tanker had run aground. Mandy was strong for her age, and fit. I watched the long smooth muscles in her thighs draw and tauten when she climbed the tumbled rocks ahead of me. The sun caught small golden hairs on her legs and arms and I found myself wondering how they would feel under my touch. She caught my eye and smiled softly.

When we paused at the edge of the rocks to catch our breath the tall prow of the wreck was level with our feet. The sea was calm and clear, the water pushing and bulging against the dark bulk of the wreck.

I had scuba'd with my wife on this wreck one summer. We chose a day at slack tide when the southeaster had blown for days and the sea was swept so clean, visibility was a good forty feet. We'd entered the water hard by the rocks and descended to twenty feet and found a gash in the tanker's prow that had split the hull in two, and we were able to swim from port to starboard inside the wreck and emerge into dappled underwater sunlight on the far side. Inside the wreck we paused and when my eyes adjusted to the gloom I saw high above us a dark companionway. I swam up to it and looked in. There was no light, no movement but the shifting of darkness on shadow. I beckoned my wife to join me but she shook her head. Ever since, I had wondered what lay on the other side of the dark companionway where she would not follow me.

In clear water on the far side again, looking back towards the stern, the wreck disappeared into the blue gloom like a great dead whale, the rudder poised in deep water that stretched uninterrupted to South America. But my wife was silent after the dive and would not speak about the wreck and refused to dive on it with me again; nor did I ever discover what had so affected her. I often thought that she had been afraid to look beneath the surface into that shadowy under-world for fear of unknown creatures that waited there to ambush her. I wondered what Mandy would make of it.

She stripped quickly down to her black Speedo and I saw again the arrogant beauty of her young body. There was no androgeny, despite her youth. I undressed to my swim trunks and as I pulled on my wetsuit pants I sensed she was watching me.

'Do you play a lot of sport?'

'Not any more,' I said, shrugging on my wetsuit top. 'Why?'

'Where did you get your muscles from?'

'I did a bit of gymnastics at school, nothing special. Athletics, rugby, cricket, the usual,' I shrugged. 'Why?'

'I don't like to look at men who don't have strong muscles. Neither does Mummy, I know. She pretends she likes those skinny boys who look like girls but she doesn't really. Nor do I. Golly! How did you get that huge scar on your arm?'

'Car accident,' I lied. I zipped up my wetsuit. Perhaps one day I would tell her about the elephant.

'And what's that cross you're wearing?'

I touched the Tuareg cross that the old woman had given me all those years ago.

'A woman gave it to me.'

'A girlfriend?'

'No.'

'Just a friend?'

'Yes.'

'It's beautiful.'

'It's very old. She said it was magical.'

'Did she? How?'

34

'Makes you wise.'

'Are you wise?'

'Not yet.'

I kept a careful eye on her as she prepared for the dive but she was reassuringly meticulous. There was an expression of suppressed excitement in her eyes. She dangled her flippers in the water and said, 'Come on Paul, the sea won't wait forever.'

I sat beside her and explained the layout of the wreck and we planned the dive together. She was impatient. 'Listen to me, you little wretch,' I said. 'There's an old saying: Plan the dive for safety –'

'– and dive the plan safely,' she chorused. 'I've heard all that.'

'Okay smartass, have you heard this one? "There are old divers, and there are bold divers; but there are no old, bold divers."' She rolled her eyes at me. 'Come on, please. Please.'

'And don't ever get out of my sight. Not for a second. This is a steel wreck. There are jagged plates everywhere and it's dangerous. And watch out for fishing line right here at the edge. I've been snagged before and it's almost impossible to get free.'

Together we slid into the water. It was cold and clear. She gave me the circled thumb and forefinger sign which means "everything okay" in scuba language and we duck-dived and swam slowly to the sandy bottom thirty feet below. I watched to see if she compensated properly for the increased pressure on her eardrums. Sunlight writhed and flickered across the sand.

Out of the corner of my eye, at the very fringe of vision, I saw dark shapes edge close then flicker away. Dolphins? Sharks? I took Mandy's hand and pulled her towards to me. Her eyes behind the glass of her mask were surprised. I squinted into the silent blueness. Images shifted and shivered. There are sharks even in the coldest of the Cape waters and I didn't want to provoke an attack. The long towering stems of the giant kelp bed swayed rhythmically in the swells. There were no more shadows in the gloom.

Satisfied, I released Mandy's hand and we swam up to the wreck and I stretched out my hand and touched the rusted steel hull. Bright green weed waved as the swells heaved above us.

I indicated the huge jagged gash in the hull before us, checked to see that Mandy was relaxed and pulled myself inside the wreck. It was dark but sunlight showed bright through the jagged tear on the far side. I turned and watched Mandy's exhalations plume out from her demand valve in a long surprised stream of bubbles. Her eyes were bright with excitement. Below, two mottled green crayfish quested at us with long antennae. I stretched out a hand and with a hunchbacked contraction of its tail the larger darted out of range.

I took Mandy's hand and pulled her up towards a bulkhead where the dark companionway I'd seen on my dive with Eva opened onto the next deck. Our exhalations collected in fat silver masses on the decaying deck above us and quivered like jellyfish. We peered through the cascading stalactites of rust and weed that framed the companionway. On an impulse I swam through the narrow opening and down to a rectangular hatch below. Pillars of sunlight seeped through from the shattered superstructure above. A ladder beckoned me downwards, and knowing I was breaking the rules, knowing I was taking a bad risk, knowing I could get us hopelessly lost, I led Mandy down into the darkness.

We found ourselves in a vast empty hold lit only by thin bars of shifting light that came and went with the movement of the sea. A tangle of metal – spars, stairs, piping, twisted girders, a row of small boilers, stove-in cylinders and a jumble of unidentifiable steel rubbish – filled the huge area.

We began to explore. The movement of our flippers stirred up silt from the deck and we became slowly shrouded in a fine mist of rust, sand, organic matter and dirt. Our exhalations streamed out like wraiths and soared upwards to be trapped by the roof. A small shoal of blacktail dassies, moving as one, flickered towards us, paused with incurious eyes and passed on, the black saddles on their caudal peduncles flirting in the dark blue shadows.

I was full of a strange anxiety and realized that the wreck felt actively malefic. When you dive you are continually aware of the muscular flexing of the sea all about you, but here in this great submarine room the water was quiet and still as if waiting. I also sensed a distant metallic groaning, a keening as of steel teeth in rote against each other as the huge riveted plates of the tanker's hull strained taut against the shouldering of the waves. As my eyes grew accustomed to the darkness, I saw the hold was lined by watertight doors – some closed, some half-open, some hanging awry – that led to unknown sections of the tanker, inhabited by unseen sea-creatures that lived forever in darkness, waiting for prey to pass.

I kicked upwards to clear the mist and looked around for Mandy but she was gone. No bubbles, no sign of her. I felt panic rise. My eyes darted everywhere. Nothing. Silly little shit, where was she? If she got lost in the wreck she'd die. Think. I decided to search each of the open doors in turn. I started on the port side, swinging the first door wide on rusted hinges, and looked inside. No rising silt, just darkness. Next door: nothing, nor the next, nor the next, nothing on the port side, no sign at all. I swam the width of the tanker, feeling a terrible dread, and hopelessly searched the dozen open doors there. Nothing.

The darkness stared back at me. I checked my diving watch: bottom time thirty-five minutes. My pressure gauge told me I had only 500 psi of air left: five minutes maximum at that depth, even if I tried skip-breathing. Panic rose in my gullet like vomit.

Then I saw a circular opening in the deck below, half covered by fallen girders and a collapsed entanglement of metal debris. I swam over and peered in. The rusted conduit led downwards like a diseased colon into a dim half-lit half-world. A trace of silt hung suspended in the water. I kicked down and found myself in a small oppressive chamber. A narrow opening showed pale against the dark. I tried to swim through but my tank snagged against the steel. I pushed hard against the bulkhead but I was stuck fast. Panic again. What a stupid way to die. Despite the icy water I felt the sweat of fear start all over my body, hot inside my wetsuit. Think.

Think: if you die the child dies too. Then I remembered my training. Snagged tank: undo webbing, shrug off tank keeping DV in mouth, hold tank, clear snag, replace tank, proceed. I removed the tank, eased the DV first stage and tap out of the steel jaw of the bulkhead rim and, pushing the tank ahead of me through the opening, swam through to the far side.

I was in another of the seemingly endless steel compartments. I shrugged my shoulders into the harness and peered through the opening on the far side of the steel cell. Mandy was in the next compartment, her blond hair floating as lightly as a mermaid's, suspended motionless and weightless in the quiet water, peering intently at a seashell she held in her hand. Calm bubbles streamed from her DV. My own DV was feeding me air in ragged sips now. The needle of my pressure gauge was firmly in the red. I banged my dive knife angrily against my tank to attract her attention and her head turned quickly at the metallic ringing. Incredibly, she was grinning at me. I beckoned her to me and she swam obediently to my side. Taking a firm grip on her wrist, I turned and led her through the chain of compartments, up through the shattered hold, out of the tangled maze of steel and finally to the surface.

When we stood together safely on the rocks I was shivering with cold and panic.

'What the hell do you think you were doing, you silly little shit,' I said, and shook her. 'You could've killed us.'

She stared at me with wide eyes.

'You frighten me when you're angry,' she said. 'I've never seen you angry before.'

'Diving is not a game, nor an adventure,' I said, feeling the anger drain away, knowing I was angry with myself for putting us at risk.

'I'm sorry.'

'And I'm sorry I shouted,' I said. 'It was my fault really.'

'No,' she said. 'It was mine. You don't know about me and the sea yet.' I didn't know what to say to that. We packed the dive-bags and she put her hand in mine for comfort as we walked. It felt as fragile as a small bird.

By the time we reached the cottage she had regained her self-possession, although she sensed something had happened to us and between us underwater that she could feel but not articulate. To cover this confusion she demanded a hot bath and supervised the running of it to make sure the temperature was to her liking. When her bath was run, she turned to me and said: 'I'm sorry I frightened you in the wreck. I was careless and you were worried about me. I'm sorry.' It was a very mature speech, I thought.

'That's okay,' I said.

'And another thing. I want to thank you for this,' she said softly. 'For the dive. I've never felt anything like it; I felt like I wasn't diving in the sea at all; I felt like I was diving in myself and into you and into the sea all at the same time.'

I watched her.

'And something else,' she said. 'I made you sad, and I don't want to do that. I've seen how sad you look sometimes when you think I'm not looking, and I don't want you to be sad. I'll make it up to you. I want to make you happy.'

'I'm not at all sad,' I protested.

'Yes you are', she said. 'Come on, I'll race you to the outside shower.'

We stripped off our wetsuits on the porch and washed them in fresh water under the outdoor shower, screened from prying eyes on the beach by a shoulder-high stone wall. Mandy was squealing and shrieking at the cold. As she leapt and danced in the spray I saw that her black swimming costume had pulled aside slightly to reveal softly-curled dark blond hair in her groin. I looked away.

She sensed immediately that my mood had changed. Shivering, her arms covered in goosebumps, she looked up at me.

'What's wrong?'

'Nothing.'

'There is, I can tell.'

'Nothing. Go and bath.' She gave me a piercing last look and ran inside. I stood and looked at the sea. This was not what I had expected. Somehow, until that instant, she had been a little girl to me, half-woman perhaps, wholly inviolable. How could a glimpse of that most laughable of human characteristics, a pubic tuft, change the way I thought of her? Did I sense menstrual blood, did I intuit a receptivity, a slickness of vaginal lips now? It was pathetic.

'Paul,' she called from indoors.

'What?'

'Come and wash my back.'

'Don't be ridiculous.'

'Please?'

'No.'

'Please?'

I ignored her but felt a little trapped. She had sensed the change in me instantly. And I knew that I was now on the defensive.

'Paul?'

'Yes, what?'

'I need a towel.'

'There is a towel.'

Silence.

'Paul?'

'Yes, what?'

'You can come in, I'm out of the bath.'

I walked inside. She was not in the sitting room. 'Where are you?'

'Here . . .' her voice called from the bedroom. Unsuspecting, I walked through and saw her standing there, wet hair pinned clumsily on top of her head, dressed in a black lace teddy that had once belonged to my wife. I would like to say that I turned around and left the room immediately, but I didn't. Her mouth looked fuller, her eyes soft and dark and watchful.

'I said I would dress for you today . . .' she said very quietly. I looked at her body: the strawberry nipples beneath the lace, her little breasts like swollen ducks' eggs, the incurve of her pubis with its smudge of hair, the pale fire that ran in highlights down her thighs. She moved towards me and a tendon drew and relaxed in her groin as she walked. Pulled tight, the lace divided her labia. I wanted to say, Go away, stop this, leave me, go home and stop the teasing, but I said nothing. She stood in front of me, hands at her sides, and watched me. I could smell her: a perfume of seawater, bathsoap, the fresh-mushroom scent of her wet unplundered vulva. I wanted to go down on my knees and slide my tongue into that savoury cleft, lick her to orgasm, feel her taut ecstatic contractions on my lips, but I did not.

I was saved by the memory of myself in the mirror. Clarity and sanity returned. The whole thing was ridiculous. I stepped back and away from her. She watched me intensely.

'Go away, Mandy,' I said very gently. 'This won't work, it won't work.'

'But I like you so much . . .'

'Mandy: I'm thirty six; you're fourteen, it's impractical, illegal and immoral.'

'Just hold me then.'

'No.'

'You're scared.'

'Of course I'm scared. You're very – attractive.'

'Really?'

'You know that.'

'One of Daddy's friends said I was sexy. He invited me to tea.'

'Did you go?'

'Just the once.'

'And?' I asked, all prurient interest and jealousy.

'He kissed me for a long time and I enjoyed it so much I told all my friends and one of them told her mother and she told my mother and she got very angry.'

'I bet. Is that why she phoned me?'

She shrugged. 'Probably ... she thinks I still see the other man.'

'Do you?'

'I saw him once. I let him pick me up after school. He put his hand up my skirt but I didn't want him to. Since then, never. But I want you to.'

'Mandy. For God's sake.'

'I do, truly. Please, Paul, just kiss me once.'

'No, Mandy. Stop it. I like you very much but this is not possible.'

She watched me carefully, her body taut. Then: 'Are you cross?'

'Of course I'm not cross.'

'Do you want me a little bit?'

'You know I do.'

She nodded, satisfied. 'I'll come and visit you tomorrow, then,' she said, and turned away. Her buttocks moved softly as she walked. She turned at the bed, looked at me with a dark smile, hooked a forefinger under one of the thin spaghetti shoulder straps of the teddy and pulled it down.

I fled.

SEVEN

By the time Mandy left it was almost four, the sun was dropping fast, and the sea had a million quicksilver tucks in it. Towards the horizon, towering anvil-shaped thunderheads reared skywards. Distant windblown rain reached down to the sea. Rainwind began to pucker the surface in my bay, setting whitecaps in the water in the shallows and making a noise like ripping silk through the single date palm behind the house.

Eva slid quietly into my mind. There'd been a similar palm in the garden of the house where she and I first lived together and the whipping fronds reminded me of the summer storms that arrived so unexpectedly then.

What gave Mandy the power to raise Eva from the grave of my past? Perhaps she had come to persuade me to face the truth at last. And Eva was both truth and untruth, the way back to my past. To face the past was to face Eva.

Eva was one of those creamy blondes who look their best wearing lipstick the colour of drying blood. Languid, graceful, her breasts full, the aureoles of her nipples soft, full-blown, veined delicately blue beneath the thin skin, eyes grey-green and direct, watchful. Hands lazy, the nails always lacquered red. Her thighs were full on the inside right at the top, firmed by swimming, shaped by early ballet classes, awaiting touch, imbued with knowledge. When I met her she was vulnerable, broken by a failed marriage, distrustful, brittle, but saved by a wonderful sense of humour and an ironical wit that I found enchanting. She also had a sharp but indolent intellect, and an archaic and frightening insight that made her often melancholic.

There was an air of great danger about her; but reading the signs wrongly, I thought the danger was directed inward. On her right wrist, beneath the cinnamon tan, there were six small vertical cicatrices of scar tissue where she had once slit each vein with great self-damning precision. She refused to tell me why; it was one of those things she kept secret, would never share. Watching her, I remember thinking: the night has teeth and she has taken them; the darkness has claws and they are hers. Physically, her daughter was a small perfect copy of her, solemn, loving, with a fierce, joyful wickedness I adored.

It was summer then and we lived in a newly-renovated terra-cotta house in a cobbled street high above the city. It was a small eighteenth century house that had once served as officers' quarters for the British garrison at the Cape and in summer the sun burnt the pigment to a pale Naples yellow but sudden rains turned the walls to the colour of sweet paprika.

In our garden stood the tall date palm and at the start of summer it began to seed in the heat, stretching out to the sun long tightly-furled spears that tautened and curved and darkened slowly from yellow ochre to tobacco in the heat. Swollen at first, the spears folded their leaves protectively in overlapping layers about their seed; but when the hot days would not end, the leaves split and burst and unfurled as if some ancient undeniable imperative had risen up through the tree from the soil; and the tree's pale seed showered out silently and full in the heat and blueness and hung suspended like ripe millet in the air.

That summer we discovered ourselves in each other. Without hurry, because we believed we had all the time in the world, we began to swim like divers into the shadows. We lived in a daze of lust and tenderness. Making my tongue drunk with a voluptuary's eagerness on the scent inside Eva's mouth; her mouth like an over-ripe fruit, the taste beyond sweetness, the juice dripping into the depths of you from the moist everted membranes of her body. Licking her where she dared not say she delighted in the licking, tonguing deep into secret clefts; her neck pale, hair wild, the sensation pressed beyond the human until the whole universe flooded out of you and into her body. When I touched her lips that summer we were all earth and sky and I was the sea driving in at her mouth, flooding her estuary. I was bird and wind together.

In our lovemaking there was a strange spiritual clairvoyance. We were sentient proof of Novalis's assertion that all absolute sensation is religious. The ecstasy of the flesh transfigured us. We became mystics of the flesh, as if our lovemaking were a fusion of some divine shadow hidden deep inside. It was this tantalizing glimpse of the possibility of ecstatic union with another being that haunted me still.

That summer, the muezzin in the old lime-green mosque in the Bo-Kaap measured out our days each morning and dusk with raw Arab quarter-tones, calling the faithful to service and I thought often of that wonderful Islamic prayer: "I praise the perfection of God, the Desired, the Existing, the Single, the Supreme; the perfection of God, the One, the Sole ... his Perfection be extolled ..."

It was all too perfect to last and I should have known that but I didn't.

But I knew we had reached the anteroom of our self-made hell one day when we were drinking coffee in the sunny sitting room of our terra-cotta house. We'd spent the previous night making love under a stalking moon. It was Sunday morning and I'd fetched croissants from the local bakery and Eva was buttering hers while we watched two hoopoos worming the lawn in the morning sunlight. We were alone; the child was visiting a schoolfriend.

'Spring!' Eva said. 'God, I love spring!'

'Moral exuberance?'

'Not only. Alive. Alivealivealive!' Then with a shriek she leapt out of her chair, spilling coffee in a golden stream into the air. Her cup shattered on the tiled floor. The saucer hit the floor on its rim and spun with a ceramic ringing round and round until it came to a gritty halt amongst the fragments of the coffee cup. I put down my cup quietly and walked over to her and took her in my arms. She was shaking.

'Are you alright?'

'Ghosts, ghosts,' she said in a frightened whisper.

'Ghosts?'

'Oh, God, yes!' she said and pushed me irritably away. 'Yes, I said ghosts.'

'Oh.'

'Don't you believe in ghosts? Why are you looking at me like that?'

'Like what?'

'Like that. Stupidly. As if I'm mad.'

'I'm not. I'm just worried,' I said gently.

'Don't shout at me. How dare you shout at me!' she screamed.

'Shout? Who's shouting?'

'You are!'

'Shouting?'

'Shoutingshoutingshouting!' she screamed and stood staring at me with wild eyes, fists clenched, mouth set. I shook my head and walked over to her and tried to hold her but she pushed me angrily away with her fists. 'Don't touch me! Leave me alone!'

'Eva,' I said. 'Please don't be stupid.'

'I'm not stupid. You're stupid. Stupid. Stupid bloody man. You never see ghosts so they don't exist, do they?' She stared at me wildly, her eyes unfocussed.

'Eva; ghosts: yes, I know about the ghosts; but I'm worried about you.'

'Worried? About me? What for? What's wrong with me? There's nothing wrong with me, but there's plenty wrong with you,' she said with a cunning little smile. I shook my head and this infuriated her because she spun and walked through to the bedroom where the child's old cot stood. To my amazement she lowered the side and climbed in and curled up around the tiny pillow and closed her eyes like a child faking sleep. I leant against the door jamb and watched her, my arms folded. She opened her eyes and stared at me with the kind of disinterested rage I once saw in the eyes of a big eagle crouched irritably on its perch at the zoo.

'What are you staring at?' she hissed. 'Why are you staring? Stop staring. Stop it!' This last she forced out between clenched teeth.

'Eva, please,' I said softly.

'Go away. I hate you. Go away.'

I waited a moment for her to retract this but she closed her eyes and held her pillow closer, pouting like a sulky child. There was nothing left to say. I turned and left the room, shutting the door very softly behind me because I wanted so badly to slam it.

Finally and most damning: she often sang when she was happy. She had a clear, pretty voice with a sad edge to it and I liked to listen to her. Sometimes the words were inaudible but often, too often, she sang a melancholic little song, half joke and half lament, constructed over centuries from the plaintive notes of ancient male grief. When I asked her, she told me it was chanted softly by men as they worked the fields up in central Africa. There were only three words, repeated endlessly in melodic variation: "... all women cheat ..."

★

There were other significant events. Late that first summer we drove nails into a small alcove in the outside walls of our house and hung up my weird little ceramic masks, bought long ago in Rome. There were five: a tragic mask, a horror mask, a smiling mask, a terror mask and the last a woman's face in half-profile with multiple Picasso-like perspectives: the face of a Venus still half-stunned from her birth in the foam.

Above them we hung Eva's one and only mask, an Inca-like face with a hooked nose and blank eyes, a mouth turned down in derision, sceptical of the whole cosmos. On the head of this priest or sacrificial victim the sculptor had placed wings and a condor's face, as if that cruel head bore its totem permanently above.

One day we saw a smiling terra-cotta sun in one of the many dark, poky little craft shops in Long Street and on an impulse bought it to reign above our pantheon of masks. At dusk, with the muezzin calling, I climbed a rickety ladder and nailed the fat-cheeked sun in place at the very top. He sat very well there and when we later found a similar blue-enamelled moon, I felt that our cosmos was complete. Satisfied, we toasted our constellation of personae in rough Portuguese wine. I often went outside to ponder this cluster of masks; they seemed to be replete with arcane meaning, like a complex poem, but for the life of me I could not tease that meaning out.

There were hints, hints followed by guesses. That autumn, late one afternoon, our sun fell with a crash and broke into so many fragments I could not repair it. The child was heartbroken, and I felt unaccountably sad, but Eva said nothing. And although I searched hard and questioned all the drunks who sunned themselves outside the Palm Bottle Store beside the mosque under the twin Long Street palms, and despite my interrogating all the Malay families who had lived in that area for centuries, I was never able to find the shop where we first bought the sun, nor have I ever found another since.

★

I have often wondered if I could have predicted the decay of our love, but I cannot answer. All I know is that our love seemed holy, ordained by logos, blessed by Eros, sacred, impersonal and complete. At one time, I believed we had snatched permanence from the flux, had cheated the wheeling cosmos and the darkness between the stars, but that was vanity. I should have been warned. And after all, I was not unprepared.

I had long cherished a Latin inscription I found on a painting of St Sebastian by Mantegna, a dark, sad line occluded by oxidised paint: 'Nothing is stable unless divine; the rest is smoke ...' ... Nihil nisi divinum stabile est; caetera fumus ...

So perhaps I should have guessed. We had many cats at our terra cotta house, mischievous females and indolent males who bred with a ferocity that was truly astounding. Naturally, the mortality rate amongst the kittens was high and each death brought with it a fresh outburst of grief from the child. I decided that a full burial service might bring catharsis and together we wrapped the tiny corpses in Eva's scarves, collected petals to scatter and dug small graves in the soft soil beneath our paw-paw trees. There, our trowels grated on bone: femurs, tibias, fibulas, vertebrae and even a skull. We were living on top of an old charnel house. The child was intrigued, her mother smiled her dark enigmatic smile, and I knew at last why the house felt so full of contending spirits.

Now, standing here on this silent beach, the child gone, love gone, I could think only of the lone gull I saw pinned against the wind, and watching it I thought: Ah, the wind has changed. And indeed it had, swinging round to the southeast, bringing clear skies. It would be a lovely day tomorrow. Perhaps she would come back tomorrow.

EIGHT

When I woke I found a clouded morning sky all silver and black like a fresh mullet. It was a fine sky to wake up to.

It was only seven o' clock and I'd sat with Ludwig, fed him his chicken and tablets and was sitting on the porch with my morning coffee, watching the sea. The air smelt of kelp, as if it had lain too long in an underwater cave. There was a thin seamist that would burn off by eight and I could feel the heat coming. It would be one of those blue enamelled days: enamelled sky, enamelled sea, the air humid at dusk.

Far along the beach I saw a lone figure walking, fetched my binoculars and watched Lockhart as he trudged towards my cottage through the soft powder sand, fishing rod over his shoulder, a screaming cloud of steel-grey gulls whirling around his head. He was wearing an old pair of khaki trousers and a blue jersey.

I wondered if he'd ever been married. I knew so little about him. Who was the woman who visited him at dusk and left, like a guilty revenant, well after midnight each month? Mother, wife, sister, lover, daughter, friend? In his wild years – about which he never spoke – had he ever been tempted by the seductive glory of the here-and-now? Had he ever been lured from his quest by the distractions of the flesh? What was that quotation from St. John of the Cross he'd once murmured? '. . . the soul cannot be possessed of the Divine Union until it has divested itself of the love of created beings . . .' If I could only divest myself of my love for Eva.

I lowered my binoculars and went inside to brew fresh coffee. When I returned to the porch he was already sitting comfortably in one of my old wood-and-canvas camp chairs.

'Good morning Paul,' he said when he heard my footsteps. 'Lovely morning.'

'Hello Lockhart. Sleep well?'

'Always.' I don't know why, but I felt he was lying. 'And you? What little escapades have you been up to?'

'Nothing much. Ludwig's sick.'

'I'm sorry. What is it?'

'A stroke, the vet says,' I said, pouring coffee and handing him a steaming cup. He likes his coffee hot.

'Thank you. I had a Labrador once, my guide dog. Wonderful dog. Guided me for, oh, ten, twelve years. Wonderful dog. That lovely wheaten colour, I was told. So eager to help. And loyal; intelligent, too. He died of a stroke, broke my heart.' He sipped his coffee. 'This is good, what is it?'

'Kenyan. A friend brings me beans from Nairobi.'

He nodded, murmured: 'The dog, the dog . . .'

'What about the dog?'

'It was impossible for me to believe that dog had no soul. One of my earliest schismatic acts, I fear.'

'Schismatic? You're a Catholic?' I asked in surprise.

'Don't be absurd,' he said sharply. 'Too rigid, too dogmatic, too . . .'

'You're an agnostic? Naughty Lockhart.'

'Quite.' He smiled: 'Wouldn't do to doubt God. What if he reciprocated?'

'Yes . . .' I said, wondering if that's what had befallen me. 'Was that your first . . . diabolical act?' I asked.

'Diabolical? No,' he said very quietly. 'There was one earlier, and rather more serious, I fancy.'

I waited for him to enlarge but he remained silent. Then: 'And what about the girl?'

'Girl? What girl?'

He watched me – if that is possible for a blind man – and waited.

'Oh, you mean Mandy,' I said casually.

'Do I?'

'Yes.'

'Mandy, is she?'

'Yes, Mandy. How did you know?'

'I smelt a new perfume around the place.'

'Ma Griffe . . . Eva wore it too.'

'It's on your jersey. And this new woman?'

This was dangerous ground. 'I fear I have failed the good lord yet again,' I said softly, watching two sandpipers scurry on hurried feet up and down the tideline, pecking at shiny black mussels.

'Oh, yes?'

'Yes ... she's only fourteen.'

'Dear me. And?'

'Nothing. Nothing physical, anyway. She came to see Ludwig at first.'

'And then?'

'Stayed to visit me. I'm not encouraging her.'

'Nor rejecting her?'

'No. I'm trying to be morally neutral.'

'My dear boy, there's no such state!' He laughed softly. 'This is typical of the Old Man, isn't it?' He sometimes referred to his god in this way, or perhaps he meant the devil. 'You couldn't've anticipated temptation from this quarter, could you? One never does.'

'No other woman would've got past my defences.'

'Woman?'

'Well, she is part, almost, nearly.'

'But a child still.'

'I don't know ... there's something ...'

'Odd?'

'No. Yes. I don't know.' I felt very uncomfortable. 'It's as if, almost, as if she'd been my child before; or as if we share some extremely ancient blood-link.' I made a helpless gesture. He nodded.

'And it's wrong for the child to love me?'

'Does she?'

'I think so.'

'Wrong for whom? You? The child?'

'Morally?'

'No, I think not. But there are ... impediments to spiritual knowledge in this affection for another's flesh. Even unacted,' he added with a wry smile and quoted: '"Whosoever looketh on a woman to lust after her hath committed adultery with her already in his heart ..." But not to you, you're a pagan, aren't you? Like me. You don't have to wreak retribution on your-

50

self, blind yourself so you can no longer look in lust, pluck out your eyes to save your soul.'

'Am I? Are you? What does that mean? Is that what you did?'

'You worship a different god. Gods,' he replied, ignoring my question.

'Wrong gods?'

He sighed. 'From my dreary ascetic perspective, yes. From the jolly old church's, yes. But from God's? Who knows. More schism.'

'Can't pagans sin?'

'Interesting question. Only against their own codes I suppose.'

'Not against their gods?'

'Which gods might those be, dear boy?'

'Poseidon,' I said, I don't know why.

'Poseidon, eh? Interesting. Your name, Morgan, means "man of the sea." Did you know that?'

'No. So?'

'I don't know.'

'I do,' I said. 'I often think I've sinned against a whole pack of gods, Poseidon included. And Eros-'

'Ah! There –'

'Lust's no good?'

'Not without love. Sometimes you remind me of what Eliot said about John Donne.'

'I don't recall.'

'". . . who saw no substitute for sense to seize and clutch and penetrate . . ."'

I was beginning to tire of this hair-splitting but before I could say anything he went on: 'You must divest yourself-'

'– I know: of the love of created beings. That's all very well,' I said, 'but there's something very pure about lust, it's honest. I feel validated by it. Felt. It's not terribly common since Eva left, which is why the child's such a nuisance.'

'I grasp that, Paul. Only too well.'

'Making love to Eva, I felt I was praying. Do you have the faintest idea what that means Lockhart? Do you?'

'Yes,' he said mildly.

'And another thing: I think being whole is much more important than being good.'

'Yes, I know you do.'

He reached into his pocket and held out a seashell to me. 'What is it?'

'A rather dull cone shell,' I answered. 'Why?'

'Have you ever cut one open?'

'No. Why?'

'I did once, vertically, when I was young. Inside, that rather dull shell as you call it is plated with mother of pearl; there are ellipses of nacre, a structure that's mathematically pure, exquisitely beautiful.'

I stared at him in surprise. It was the longest speech he'd ever made.

'And?'

'And I think the universe is like that,' he said softly. 'Dull and ordinary on the surface, but underneath! A metaphysical geometry of great and profound beauty. All my life I have tried to intuit that beauty.'

'And?'

He smiled wryly. 'No luck so far.'

'I suppose that's where we differ,' I said slowly. 'There's nothing remotely dull about the universe to me.'

'But so superficial. And such distractions,' he said pointedly.

I returned the shell to him and he stowed it away in his pocket.

'And because you suspect this hidden order exists, it's naughty for me to lust after women?' I said harshly.

He nodded.

We sat in silence. I looked at the sea. No doubt Lockhart sensed my irritation. After a time he said gently: 'How about a little of that Beethoven you like so much?'

'Those quartets? Yes.' I went inside, found Opus 132, put it on and turned up the volume. The strange pre-Christian harmonies filled the room, overflowed onto the porch, crept across the waters. We sat together and listened. This was direct confrontation with the godhead, hard-won, without dogma, without strictures or prohibitions.

When the music ended I felt its temporary serenity pass into silence. After a time Lockhart said, ' I'm sorry to do this, but I must ask you a question.'

'Of course.'

'There is a new bleakness in you. Why?'

'"Teach us to care and not to care,"' I said.

'Yes?' He pondered. Then: 'You know, you're not the first person to lose your wife, to lose at love. And self-pity doesn't become you.'

'I know, Lockhart. But this is different. This time I'm empty and alone and without faith.'

He nodded reflectively, being extremely polite, then said: 'You know, we cannot all be saints. The way of the saint is the way of the saint precisely because sainthood is already part of that person's nature.'

'Go on.'

'Our job in the here-and-now, in my opinion—no, you don't want to hear this.'

'I do, actually.'

'Our job is to discover our true nature, our self, and be that.'

'This isn't precisely new.'

'No; Hopkins and the Gnostics said it often. But what if your longing for spiritual perfection is not real, not true, but an escape, a sham? What if the child is here to show you that?'

I shifted uneasily, stood up from my chair, poured cold coffee, drank it. I'd predicated my future on knowing God, on knowing the whole universe with my flesh. 'I don't know,' I said.

'Don't want to know?' he queried softly.

I shook my head, not that he could see. 'I don't think your way is my way,' I said.

He nodded. 'You may be right. I'm not sure my way is my way any more.'

He stood up, felt for his rod and his bait-box and carefully descended my steps. He turned at the green glass fishing buoy, salvaged long ago, and said, 'Goodbye, Paul. How about some fishing? I can't tomorrow, but how about the day after?'

'No, I can't. I've people coming to lunch.'

'Nice or bloody?'

'Bloody nice. An old friend of mine from university: Charles. One of my lecturers. And his boyfriend,' I added, to see what he'd do.

'Sodom and Gomorrah,' he said equably.

'Do you want to come?'

'No, thanks.'

'You're more than welcome Lockhart.'

'I know that; but I'd just put them off their feed. Disturb their universe.' He waved goodbye.

As he turned away a thought struck me. 'Did you catch anything today?'

'Not this morning, not even a cold,' he smiled, and walked off down the beach. The gulls began to flock around him again and I saw his hand go into the bait box and then he was throwing small pieces of redbait into the air. The gulls began to scream and fight, twisting and diving. I watched him out of sight.

NINE

She did not come at all that day and I paced the house and stared at the sea, waiting. At dusk I felt justified in drinking a small gin and tonic to celebrate the sunset. That I followed by another, and another and another until, by midnight, the bottle was empty and I fell asleep on the couch in a dribbling drunken stupor with all the lights on.

I woke next morning with the early sun hot on my face. I just made it to the lavatory and retched up several gallons of gin and a vile string of yellow bile until my stomach muscles ached. There was only one cure. I walked unsteadily down to the beach and dived into the shallows, feeling the velvet iciness of the sea close over my head. It took a good half hour of determined swimming but finally I felt human and ran shivering up the beach to the house to check on Ludwig.

She did not come at eight, nor nine. I put on the Art of the Fugue and listened absentmindedly to the plaited harmonies. Ten o' clock came and went and the sun was rising high and hot before I heard her tapping at my glass doors. I walked through from the porch and saw her face pressed against the glass, one hand cupped close to cut out reflections. She grinned at me, all gleaming teeth. She was wearing white shorts, a dark blue t-shirt and plimsolls. She looked nautical.

'Hello, Paul!' She skipped to me to be hugged. I caught her at arms' length, squeezed her shoulders in a brotherly way and released her.

'You're a bit late,' I said.

'Am I? Sorry. Only one day. I had things to do.'

'You could've phoned.'

She stared at me, saying nothing.

'What's in your basket?' I asked lamely.

'Beach towel, Ambre Solaire, my book, my Walkman, chicken for Ludwig, how is he? And a salad for you. What's that awful music? Beethoven?'

'Bach. Awful?'

'Awful!' She carried her laden basket through to the kitchen and transferred closed plastic containers to my fridge.

'What's in those?'

'I made a seafood salad for you.' she replied. 'You'll see. I dived out crayfish yesterday, and I picked some fresh mussels from my secret bed and pickled them, and I put in calamari and fresh tuna, too.' There was a bulky bundle at the bottom of her basket, beneath her beach clutter, wrapped in a pale blue silk shawl. I wondered what it was.

'You shouldn't dive alone,' I said. ' The water's treacherous here.'

'Not where I dived. I've got a special place in that little inlet just past Bakoven that nobody knows about and it's very calm there and not deep and all the crayfish are half asleep. How's Ludwig?'

'A bit better, I think. I took his basket outside earlier. He likes the sun.'

'Are his bowels working normally?'

'Yes, doctor.'

'Shut up, I'm interested. And his nose?'

'Wet. And yours?'

'Shut up! Is he in the pantry?'

'Yes.'

She sat beside Ludwig, talking softly and stroking his ears. His eyes closed in desperate ecstasy. He'd always loved having his ears stroked, even as a tiny puppy.

'Would you like something to drink?'

'What have you got?'

'Most things. Fruit juice? Coke?'

'A gin and tonic, please.'

'No.'

'No? Why?'

'Too strong for you.'

'Mummy lets me have one sometimes.'

'I'm not mummy. Wine?'

'Yes, please. White with soda?'

We sat outside on sunbeds in the shade of my bright yellow umbrella and sipped our drinks. The first sip was hard for me but after that my hangover vanished and I began to enjoy the day. The sky was blue as an iris; the sea translucent in the shallows where small waves broke close to the hot shore, blue with violet shadows further out, merging at the horizon into a sky that darkened to Prussian blue above us. Mandy had changed into a small black bikini and pinned up her hair. She put on a pair of RayBans and sitting there sipping her spritzer she looked like a grown woman. She had a deeply indented navel and when she stretched her arms above her head in pleasure at the heat of the sun it tautened into a vertical slit like a second vulva.

I watched a droplet of sweat form in her armpit and slide down her ribcage, past her waist and into her costume bottom. I could taste its salt on my tongue. The glare of the sun on her body was blindness in the middle of the day, she filled my eye, and I watched a narrow rim of darkness slowly surround her body, as if her secret shadow-soul had escaped her tight flesh. Then I blinked and it was gone.

'I love the sun, don't you,' she said, moving her sunbed further out of the shade.

'Yes. Don't get too burnt. The sun's terribly strong today.'

'Please will you put some oil on my back then?'

'Of course. Turn over.'

She rolled onto her stomach, buttocks clenching and relaxing, deftly unsnapped her bikini top and cradled her face on folded arms. I knelt beside her and poured a little Ambre Solaire between her shoulder blades and began to spread it over her back, offering a brief prayer to all pagan gods not to allow me to embarrass myself.

'Mmmm. That's good,' she murmured and clenched her bottom.

'Stop it, Mandy.'

'But it feels wonderful. Do my shoulders please.'

I obediently kneaded the small trapezius muscles, firm and strong.

She began making soft murmurs of pleasure. Until now, I'd managed to avoid touching her. This was difficult: in the pitch of her waist, just above her bikini bottom, there was a small patch of soft, shining blond hairs. Under a lover's touch,

I knew they would slowly stand erect. I doused them thoroughly with oil and stolidly rubbed her back in what I hoped was an uncaressive way.

'There. Done,' I said, wiping my hands on my towel.

'Thanks, that was wonderful. Shall I do you now?'

'No,' I said hurriedly. I lay back on my sunbed and closed my eyes. I felt a little nonplussed, in a way I had not since pimply adolescence. Why was this child back again? Was Lockhart right? Was I supposed to send her away, untouched, as law and society demanded?

'Don't you have any friends?' I asked.

'Yes,' she said in a sun-thickened voice. 'Lots. Why?'

'Where are they?'

'At home, gone to movies, at the beach, I don't know, who cares?'

'Don't you want to spend more time with them?'

'No.'

'Why not?'

'I see them every day at school in term time. And every night. I'm a weekly border at St. Michael's, I told you.'

'But don't you want to see more boys of your own age?'

'No. They're stupid.'

'How?'

'They want to kiss me all the time. They're just stupid.'

'I see,' I said, not seeing at all.

'I like to be with you,' she said. 'Why can't you see that?'

Why indeed? It was a good question. 'I don't know,' I said.

'I like the things we do together,' she explained. 'Talking. Ludwig. Diving; I love what I felt when we dived on the wreck, I told you. Swimming. Eating. You teach me things and I like the way you smell and I like being near you. I like it when you touch me. And I like dressing up for you. Do you like it?'

Should I lie?

I said nothing.

'Good ... shall we do it later?' she asked in a voice sleepy with heat.

I said nothing.

'Good,' she murmured.

I turned to look at her body, feeling my scrotum tighten as if in fear. Then I fell asleep, drugged by the sun.

I woke to find Mandy half-lying beside me on the sunbed, her head resting on my chest, hair tickling my nose.

'Please don't move,' she said softly. 'Just lie here. Please?'

'Mandy-'

'Please?'

So I lay there feeling slightly ridiculous, aware of her sunhot body, soft pressures and textures, a rancid edge of sun-curdled Ma Griffe, Ambre Solaire, sweat, and her heart chanting a two-part canon with mine. Her breathing was deep and slow. We lay there together for three hundred heartbeats, I counted them. Then she said in the same soft, sleepy voice, 'I'm sorry I didn't come to see you yesterday, but I'll make it up to you now. I'm going inside. Wait ten minutes, then come ...'

I neither nodded nor denied her as she slid away; I just lay there, incapable of moral judgement, bereft of moral scruples. I tried to blame the sun: lying there, the heat and light seemed to mutate sensation and thought. I was in a crucible of heat, inner and outer; I could feel the insistent tugs of temptation, this way and that, as of currents undersea, but was wholly incapable of moral action. Then I got up and stretched and walked inside and through to the bedroom, where I knew I'd find her. It was action of a sort.

Mandy had drawn the blinds so that the room was in shadow. She was standing beside the bed, fully dressed, but not in her T-shirt and shorts. She was wearing my wife's pearl-silk blouse, her dark blue silk wrapover skirt, black stockings and a pair of high black shoes that had not belonged to Eva. She must have brought them in her basket, along with her makeup: her mouth was rouged a little with lipstick, her eyes darkened with kajol. Her hair hung loose. She was Eva but not Eva; my wife but not my wife.

'Do you like me?' she asked softly.

'Yes, I like you. But this is not right ...'

'Lie down on the bed.'

'Mandy-'

'Please, I want you to.'

'Mandy ...'

'Don't speak. Lie down ...'

59

Still drugged, I did. She walked to the middle of the room and turned to face me. Then, her eyes fixed on mine, she began slowly to unfasten the buttons of the blouse. How did she know? She was not Eva, but she knew.

'Mandy . . .' I said in quiet warning, but she shook her head and shrugged off the blouse and let it fall. Underneath she was wearing an oyster satin bra, not Eva's, pale with highlights. Her little nipples were swollen. I looked away but she called me back:

'Paul . . .' and I looked back and watched her turn away from me, undo the tied belt of the silk skirt and let it fall. The suspenders and black stockings framed her bottom. I felt ashamed watching her, fascinated, shy, rapt. The cleft of her buttocks was clear through the black silk of my wife's panties. She looked at me once over her shoulder with a stripper's knowing grin then turned back to me, her eyes fixed on mine, and walked close, her stockings making a crisp hiss with each step, a naked sybilline smile on her face.

She knelt beside me on the bed, reached over and handed me one of the black sleeping masks Eva and I always kept in the bedside drawer. What she said then set a small chill on my skin, because she could not possibly have known that this was one of the small erotic games Eva and I had played: you must be blind in order to see . . .

'Put it on.'

'What?'

'Put it on.'

Eerie memories. I did. I felt her slight weight move onto the bed beside me, heard the rustle of silk on nylon.

'Do you know what I've done,' she whispered.

'No.'

'I've taken off the bra and the panties but I'm still wearing the stockings. And the shoes . . .' I said nothing. I felt her move slightly, heard a soft quick intake of breath, and she whispered: 'Do you know what I'm doing now?'

'No . . .' Again the soft breath, then: 'I'm doing what I taught all the other girls in my dorm at school to do . . . What I only do with Poseidon . . .'

TEN

A day as hot as this always brings with it a humid dusk but tonight the air is heavy with storms as well. The sun went down through a thick white haze, the air very still, and before dusk was done the wind swung into the north, clouds began to clot together and now the thunder is starting, deep rumbles like a whale burping. It will rain soon.

Mandy has just left, walking down the beach. I watched until she disappeared; perhaps she would visit me again tomorrow. I poured a Bombay gin and tonic and went out onto the porch and sat there in the twilight and drank it. My telephone stuttered, rang, fell silent.

I looked out to sea. Venus was a blot of light through the seamist. Thunder started in the faraway clouds. Lightning shuddered in huge violet sheets in the distance and my telephone tittered again, reminding me of the time I had waited all night, when we were 'separated' yet again, for Eva to call as she'd sworn she would; but when my telephone rang and I ran to it, she was not there. It was only the lightning. Electronic frissons were scurrying down the telephone's staid printed circuits, making its inarticulate little soul ring with delight. Eva didn't call that night, nor for days afterwards and I wondered why love should be so painful. But that is unimportant, now. Eva: back again, summoned up again by Mandy.

I remembered once watching Eva put on her lipstick. She always wore a blood-coloured lipstick called 'Parisienne.' She made a wide mouth at her reflection in the mirror, small white teeth just showing, and slid the lipstick in two small precise sweeps across her lips, her concentration so intense it was as if she were sharpening an edged weapon for mortal combat.

And Mandy was so like her! The apparent accessibility, but the elusiveness behind that. I walked the porch restlessly in the dark, refilled my drink, went down to the night-time beach, the sand still warm from the sun. I stalked the littered tideline barefoot hoping there were no bluebottles. Mandy, Mandy. What to make of the things she'd done in the bedroom?

The sluttishness, the wit, the trappings of the hooker, such terrible knowledge of male weakness! The calculated teasing, the stockings and high heels, the stripper's grin ... she'd revealed less to me than when she'd worn her tiny black bikini, yet she knew intuitively the heightened eroticism of black lace and silk. And if it's so tawdry, and I know that, why is it so sexy? Why am I so weak? All I had to help me was irony, and in the face of Mandy's fleshly wisdom that was proving useless.

And again like Eva, she'd known that the sexuality of her autoerotic act was made more intense because I was blinded by my sleeping mask. But how? In the kitchen later when I asked her why she'd done that she looked at me for an instant with naughty eyes and told me she'd read it in one of Mummy's books ... And then her prayer to Poseidon: hand cupped about her swollen pudendum (I imagined) middle finger teasing her little swollen bud, sensation spreading like a paralysing drug, the mounting ecstacy, head thrown back, mouth open, tendons standing out in her neck, veins thick with longing, eyes turned up, back, inward, watching; the soft, inarticulate whimpers of disbelief: then the sudden starting of sweat all over her body – I felt its heat – and the shuddering release, the feeling of dismemberment ...

When her breathing had calmed she wriggled close to me and I felt the warmth of one small breast press against my arm and she said, 'Did you like that?' as if she was one of those ancient Dock Road whores.

And I replied, 'Yes ...' understanding nothing any more, left only with a feeling of ineffable loss and the sure knowledge that my scrotal sac was full of hot little rocks. Conundrum.

I walked back to the cottage, went inside and poured another Bombay and tonic, went out to the porch again. The air was thick with moisture, waiting. The clouds pressed down tight against the earth. Then, without warning, the rain came, roaring like a waterfall, steady and remorseless. And with it came the sudden wet smell of hot slaked dust I had last smelt up in central Africa. And suddenly I realised what Mandy was doing in my life: confronting her I was confronting my past. There was no way out or round; only through.

★

Once upon a time Eva decided we should visit her father where he lived in a remote bush camp in central Africa. He hadn't precisely ignored our marriage; he simply pretended it'd never taken place. He hadn't flown down for the small wedding and I think that hurt Eva. It was time, she now said, for her to return to the places she loved best, to the vast silent plains of yellowing grass and the quiet forests where she'd grown up.

They had great power over her, these places; and even before I knew the extent of her confused feelings for her father and Africa, I realised that our destination was the landscape of her mind, a mental construct that was more real to her precisely because it possessed all the dominating energy of myth.

An example. One drizzling Sunday we were trapped inside our beach cottage by the weather. The sea and sky were a uniform dull grey, the wind tugged at the house and quick flurries of rain scratched at the windows like lonely cats asking to be let in. Ludwig was asleep by the driftwood fire that burnt with sudden little spurts of green flame when the fire found pockets of seasalt in the grain of the logs. Eva was reading 'Out of Africa,' an old first edition given to her by her father. Abruptly she put down her book, went through to the kitchen and returned with an opened tin of mangoes.

'Mangoes,' she said with a squeal of delight. 'God, I love mangoes. Don't you love mangoes?'

'Yes, I like mangoes,' I said, looking up from my book.

'Yes, but don't you LOVE them? I LOVE mangoes.' Her voice had acquired the slight shrill edge I had come to fear.

'Mangoes are fine.'

'Fine? Fine? Mangoes aren't fine,' she said scathingly. Then, mockingly, imitating my voice in a prim, mincing tone: '"Yes, Eva, I think mangoes are fine!" God, you're thin-blooded!

Why are you so bloody stolid? Don't you ever have any JOY?'

'Not from a mango,' I said dryly.

'Bastard,' she said coolly. 'Bastard, cold-hearted bastard.' She looked at me with narrowed eyes. 'Why don't you love mangoes? I do, why don't you?'

'Yes, yes, yes, I utterly adore bloody mangoes,' I said in sudden irritation. She turned away from me with the air of quiet triumph she acquired whenever she managed to provoke me, and began to eat the slippery mango slices straight from the tin with a fork.

I watched her. Her eyes were closed and there was a small smile of absolute satisfaction on her face. And something else. Sadness? Nostalgia? Melancholy? Why melancholy? What, I thought in my brutal way, is there about fruit that can make you weepy?

Being indifferent to my own origins I could not understand homesickness and condemned it as sloppy emotionalism. I was too self-absorbed to realise that in the wild taste of the mangoes there was the whole of her African childhood: the smell of woodsmoke and tobacco on her father's bushjacket when he came home in the middle of the night from chasing marauding elephants out of some villager's shamba way up the river, bringing with him always a small, furry creature, untamed, frightened, for her to keep, a bushbaby or a genet.

She relived it: the scent of red dust slaked by rain, the conical termite mounds, the hide-and-seek game played with the small black children that set her free to run wild and hide in heart-thudding excitement until found; the smell of elephant dung, rich as fruit cake, the birds of prey turning in gyres way up in the sky, the rainclouds as dark and awesome as the wrath of god, the raindrops fatter than tears, the wet leaves, the smell of grass fires, the heat, the buffalo-horn moon, the small-footed spoor of the antelope, the sunsets the grownups never spoke of, the stars, looking at Christmas cards from relatives overseas and wondering what snow was like, and the sharp cold before dawn when she turned over in bed and pulled her blanket tight about her and wished her little girl's wish for a phantom lover to hold her in the dark.

I should have guessed. One night when we had begun to unravel our love, in the middle of one of those fights that diminish the spirit and shame both combatants, she cried out suddenly, 'Africa! I am Africa! But you aren't ... you don't understand me at all ... but Daddy does: he loves Africa ...'

She would tolerate no objection. Even when her child expressed deep sadness at being packed off to stay with a schoolfriend while we two visited Daddy, Eva, usually so tolerant and understanding, flew into a fury which made the child wide-eyed with surprise.

So to real Africa we went, to see Daddy the Great White Hunter, the noble conservationist, the legend in his own time, the uncrowned king of the bush, Dickie Coletrane.

Thinking about this, I shut up the house and went to bed. Drunk again.

PART TWO

THE BUSH

We carry with us the wonders
we seek without us.
There is all Africa
and her prodigies in us.

Sir Thomas Browne.

ONE

I saw him before Eva did. I recognised him from the photographs on the dustcovers of his books. He was waiting for us in the sweltering airport concourse when we cleared Customs and Immigration, standing under a sign that said: 'Strictly Airport Personnel Only.' A tall white-haired man, slightly stooped, with a nattily clipped white moustache, an affable smile and cold blue eyes; still broad through the shoulders and chest, wearing a neatly-pressed khaki bushjacket, khaki trousers and old leather desert boots. No socks.

'Oh, look! There's Daddy!' said Eva excitedly. She waved and he waved back, a look of innocent happiness on his face. They stared at each other, smiling, while I piled our luggage onto a lopsided squeaky-wheeled trolley and pushed it through the narrow gate guarded by a very serious-looking black policeman who suddenly smiled hugely as we passed, saying, 'You are friends of Bwana Coletrane? Welcome! Welcome ...!'

'Oh, Daddy, hello,' said Eva, hugging him tightly.

'Hello, hello.' he said, smiling. 'You look well; lovely!'

'Daddy, this is Paul,' said Eva nervously. 'My husband.'

'Hello Mr. Coletrane,' I said. 'It's nice to meet you, I've read all your books.'

'How boring for you,' he said, as we shook hands. 'Got your katundu?'

'Yes,' said Eva.

'Jolly good, let's get going, it's quite a long drive. The Land Rover's just outside.' He walked ahead, greeting several people who seemed to know him.

'What's katundu?' I asked Eva quietly.

'Katundu? Don't you know?'

69

'If I knew I wouldn't be asking.'

'Luggage,' she said shortly, and skipped happily forward to catch up with her father. She took his arm and smiled up at him. He said something to her with a wry smile that I couldn't catch, and she laughed happily. It was the first time for months I'd seen her laugh without a brittle edge to the laughter. I followed doggedly behind, pushing the luggage trolley.

I inherited from my gypsey grandmother a damning gift: I am sometimes granted terrible prescient insights, and now I knew I should not have come, that I was intruding; not that you'd need to be terribly sensitive to realize that. This time in the bush might turn out to be many things: illuminating, full of wonder, educational, exciting and stimulating. But I knew also that it would humiliate me in a manner and to a degree that already frightened me. I did not think this; I knew it as immediately as you know the scent of a rose.

I also knew that my only defence was to withdraw a little, become a little distant. In that moment I realized I understood nothing at all about Eva, nothing at all and that our savage intimacies counted for nothing, that all our dark couplings had not touched her at all. But I plodded on behind the happy couple, pondering my vision and wondering whether this trip had been such a jolly good idea, after all.

Outside in the morning heat we packed our 'katundu' on the back of the stripped down Land Rover. Eva climbed up beside her father in front, I excavated a space amongst the luggage in the back and we were away. We soon left the city and the shanty-town on its outskirts behind – avoiding goats, ancient hobbling pedestrians, cyclists and snotty-nosed children – and entered country that was hard, indifferent and inscrutable; and the longer we drove, the wilder the bush became until the tar petered out and we were on an ochre gravel road, tall trees closing in on both sides.

'What kind of trees are those?' I shouted to Coletrane over the roar of the open Land Rover. He glanced. 'Combretum, some mopane, though we only really hit that later, some lonchocarpus capassa, stand of diospyros over there ... the creepers are caparissa tomentosa, and of course those palm trees with the bulge in them are borassus, home of the Palm Swift. Do you enjoy this sort of thing?'

'Yes, very much,' I said. 'But don't these trees have common names?'

'Of course, but no point in using them.'

He turned back and began talking to Eva before I could ask why we didn't use common names.

I looked at him. His face was as wrinkled as a pickled walnut and his soft white hair fringed a balding head as brown and speckled as a new-laid egg. His eyes were the palest blue and almost hidden between his fallen upper lids and bags below so wrinkled and large they looked like those of a very old, very tired circus chimpanzee. I was reminded of Albert Einstein. The expression of kindly indifference was the same, and his smile had the same air of amused tolerance; as if he had ceased at last through distaste to wonder at his fellow-creatures' endless cruelties. But there was something else. The amused indifference turned easily to coldness, the resigned tolerance to contempt, and I had felt instantly at the airport his disapproval when he looked at me.

Perhaps this was a little unfair. But he reminded too closely of the men who were masters at my school in England, staid men who'd made war their calling, frosty men with clipped moustaches, short hair and shorter tempers; men whose icy blue eyes were distant with the Enormity of What They'd Seen Men Do; men who Distrusted the Native, and believed with arid but intense passion in the uplifting moral power of neatly folded blankets and a decent haircut.

It was clear to me that no man would ever be good enough for Eva, his only daughter; no man except a clone of Dickie Coletrane himself when young: stolid, unimaginative, courtly, obsessed by the killing of large animals and by the contents of crocodiles' stomachs. And he was accustomed to the role of relaxed paterfamilias. He expected the respect due to a father. He expected his utterances to carry weight regardless of their validity, to be accepted without serious question; and that was going to cause problems. My father died when I was very young; I had none of the inculcated respect for fatherly authority that so stunts a young man's urge to question accepted wisdom.

It was going to be an interesting time.

We passed through occasional small towns, each a clone of the last: rutted main street, the shop windows empty of goods; skinny children, beggars on broken crutches bound with filthy cloth, women breast-feeding with wrinkled empty dugs, old men sitting at the side of the road watching us with incurious eyes as we passed, sewing machines busy on the verandahs of the dark little trading stores that smelt of cheap perfumed soap, paraffin, insect spray and sweat. Tall hands of green bananas stacked beside sweet potatoes and pale bruised tomatoes, parked buses laden with passengers all talking at once, and fenced-off areas where the abandoned hulks of gutted Land Rovers, long cannibalised for spares, rusted slowly in the grass that grew up through their chassis.

Then the telephone poles stopped and the gravel road became a rutted track. We passed several villages, neat collections of bamboo-and-thatch huts in amongst scrappy palmetto; chickens, goats, small pot-bellied children who ran to the roadside to wave and smile at us, women hoeing their small plots of maize, tiny babies tied to their backs with colourful cloth.

On the journey, two strange things happened and I wasn't sure what to make of either. The first occurred when we stopped for petrol at a garage attached to a small trading store. We'd just crossed a bleak semi-desert, the floor of an ancient lake, all scrub thorn and salt-bush and blinding white sand, baking hot in the vertical midday sun. Eva had offered Daddy her sunglasses but he refused, heroically bearing the full brunt of the glare. We pulled up in the thin shade of the single dusty palm tree that served as the forecourt of the garage and the Land Rover's motor windmilled to a stop in the heat. We all got down to stretch our legs.

Wind blew dust around in little corkscrews of hot air. A Coca-Cola sign squeaked rhythmically, swung on rusted hinges by the wind. An old man in tattered overalls pushed himself reluctantly to his feet and walked slowly towards us on bandy arthritic legs. A drunken group sitting outside the store on upended boxes and an assortment of broken chairs watched us with dull eyes. A very fat woman peered round the open door of the store and waved at Coletrane. He ignored her. 'Bwana?' said the old man.

'Fill, please,' said Coletrane.

It was one of those ancient mechanical hand pumps with a long wooden arm. The old man was struggling, so I took the pump arm from him and settled into the rhythm, the smell of the petrol sharp in my nostrils. Sweat began to run off my face.

'Hello,' said Coletrane, 'here's something interesting.' I turned. An old crone was crossing the dirt road towards us where we were parked in the shade. Despite her age, she walked with a swinging, whorish tread. I watched her, half-aware of the slosh-slosh of petrol that snaked into our tank and convulsed the hose each time I swung the pump arm back and forth. The old man beside me watched her too, the smell of his multilayered sweat not unlike that of a rotting onion.

I thought at first the woman was old because she looked eccentric: a red plastic rainhat on her head, her body hung about with mongoose tails, genet skins and monkey skulls; but when she drew closer I saw her face beneath the rainhat was young, her eyes gay and direct. She carried a long wooden staff and was evidently on her way to the store behind us where the Coca-Cola sign squeaked in the wind. As she walked, the other blacks avoided her, moving quickly to one side to clear her path, their eyes lowered.

Now I could see a small smile of amusement on her face, ironical, wry, turned inward. She walked up the final shallow incline and I saw our ancient petrol attendant watching her in frightened silence. It was then that she noticed me. Her eyes fixed mine and her wry smile deepened as if we two, alone in the universe, shared the same joke, a joke that God had played on the two of us alone.

It was also a smile of enquiry; and her eyes, with their fierce direct gaze, fixed me to see if I understood. I smiled back at her and she nodded in recognition but also in agreement, as if some arcane message had passed between us, as if she saw in me another who was shunned by those who lacked all capacity for damnation. She knew she had been set aside by providence – part of that great cosmic joke again – to walk encumbered by skulls and shreds of fur and skin, the symbols of her banishment, and wished to see if I shared her knowledge of the irony.

As she smiled I saw the dusty aureoles of her small upthrust breasts point at me, naked beneath her dirt-shiny goatskin cape. She offered me a final broad, self-mocking grin, then bent her head without another look and seemed to efface herself in the throng outside the store and was gone. The Coca Cola sign squeaked rhythmically in the wind.

I had been pumping petrol automatically and as I craned around to look for her amongst the crowd I heard and smelt petrol spill into the dust. I replaced the hose, locked the petrol cap. The petrol attendant crossed himself like a devout Catholic, but I noticed he wore a fragment of vervet monkey fur bound about his wrist. He grinned at me, half in fear, I could see it in the set of his teeth.

'She mark you, boss,' he said, and giggled. 'She mark you ...'

I tried to tip him but he refused, shaking his head and pushing the money away with both hands. The crowd around the store jeered and waved empty beer bottles and urged him to accept, but he shook his head.

'Who is she?' I asked.

'She is our mnthakathi,' he said in a whisper.

'Mnthagathi?' I asked.

'Witch,' said Coletrane and started the car. Correcting my pronunciation, he said: 'Mntakathi. She's the local witch, mnthakathi. Literally, the eater of human flesh. Witch.' Eva smiled at me. I said nothing. Coletrane drove.

TWO

Shortly after, the second strange thing happened.

We were skirting the edge of a wide plain, the grass bleaching to yellow in the heat. There were clumps of acacias and I could smell a thick exotic scent in the air. I was about to ask Coletrane what it was; but when the lowering sun touched them I realized that all the acacias were in blossom, their crowns dusted with flowers the colour of lemon icing.

The smell was heady and sweet, and I spotted two big male kudu browsing on a dark green tree. Their long corkscrew horns were laid back along their flanks, their necks were thick and noble and when they turned to watch us, their ears inside were the soft pink and apricot of giant cowrie shells. I felt a sudden savage affection for them so intense that for an instant I was inside the kudu and they were part of me.

I closed my eyes tightly but the feeling would not pass. I glanced at Eva and Coletrane but they'd noticed nothing. Then I was possessed by a strange sensation: I knew the kudu were really there; but watching them I felt the surface reality, the canvas-and-pigment of them, lift just a little at the corners. And then the whole landscape – the acacias and the scent of blossom and the air and the kudu and impala and the distant trotting warthog, the vast wind-winnowed savannah and the heat-tumbled skyline – all seemed to have some hint of celestial fire at their very edge, a shimmer of energy left over from the instant of creation, a prismatic dementia of wild light that disappeared when I looked for it directly. Then the sensation was gone and I felt empty and lost and looked ahead without seeing.

The track wound in and out of the treeline as if it had lost its course. The light was almost gone. Up ahead I saw a clearing. A tall column of blue woodsmoke rose calm and untroubled through the trees. I could see tents and huts, almost hidden in the undergrowth. We drove into a small copse of ebony trees, their trunks black and twisted. Through the dark glade slanted the dusk sun. A rooster crowed somewhere. Coletrane's camp.

We rounded the last corner and there in the middle of a small clearing stood a tall black man dressed in a darned white cotton vest and long baggy khaki shorts, veritable Bombay Bloomers. The yellow light outlined his figure with a bilious halo, as if an Italian Primitive had painted a sulphurous delineating aura around a devil. At first I could not see his features but when we drove closer the light changed and I saw his face. He had about him an air of unredeemable loss and seemed distracted, as if listening to some inner voice of eternal lamentation. He was carrying in one hand a rifle that looked like a bolt-action Rigby and held five long brass cartridges in the other.

'Moni, Kalilombe,' said Coletrane, drawing up beside him.

'Moni, Bwana,' he replied in a soft voice, but his eyes were on Eva. He looked puzzled for an instant, then said with a big smile, 'Ah, dona Eva! Dona Eva! Moni! Moni!'

'Moni, Kalilombe,' she said. She chatted with him in the vernacular for a time then turned to me and said simply, 'I haven't seen him for nearly fifteen years, but now I'm home at last!' She introduced me in English. Kalilombe took my hand briefly in his dry simian paw. His eyes were blank.

His face revealed him to be nearly sixty but his body was that of a much younger man. His skin had not sagged and the pectorals I could see through the torn vest had not fallen. His legs were skinny and protruded storklike from his baggy shorts. He was barefoot and his feet were so toughened and scaly and hard they seemed to be two quite separate animals, like a pair of dusty burrowing reptiles grafted onto his ankles.

Coletrane climbed down stiffly from the driver's seat and said something questioningly in the vernacular to Kalilombe, pointing to the Rigby. Kalilombe laughed softly and spoke urgently and pointed northwards. Coletrane asked a question and made an outward, down, and insweeping gesture with both arms, in a clear attempt to mimic the great arcs of trophy-sized elephant tusks. Kalilombe nodded and laughed again and pointed to his own ribcage, low down, spoke long and intensely, pointing northwards, and making small emphatic gestures with the hand holding the cartridges.

'What are they saying?' I asked Eva.

'Kalilombe says there's a very big bull elephant that's been wounded by poachers, somewhere way up to the north. Two villagers came into camp just now and told him. Took them three days to get here. A very big bull, the kind you no longer see. Kalilombe says a hundred pounds a side. Apparently the bull's killed two of the poachers, the rest ran away. Then he chased the village women when they went down to the river to get water, caught one of them and killed her. Kalilombe's our local representative of the Game Department here, along with Daddy. They'll have to shoot the elephant to protect the locals.'

'Seems a waste . . .'

'Depends how much you value human life,' she said shortly. Kalilombe walked away, pressing cartridges down into the magazine well of the Rigby.

Coletrane turned back to us. 'Something I think you ought to see,' he said. 'Over here . . .' He led us along a faint path through the mopane to a whitewashed shed. The walls were red at the bottom where the recent rains had splashed mud onto them giving the strange illusion that the building was haemmorhaging into the earth. Coletrane pulled open the door and the smell that was released almost made me retch. The room stank of death; not individual death, but mass death. Coletrane stepped aside. 'Have a look,' he said. Eva pushed past me and peered inside.

'Ohmigod,' she said, recoiling from the smell. 'Daddy, that's awful! Look, Paul.' I looked inside. The white room was full of skulls: row upon row of rhino skulls and elephant skulls, silent and pale. Large blue flies buzzed loudly. You could see the marks on the elephant skulls where the poachers had chopped out the ivory. Some skulls had simply been bisected with chain saws. Panga gashes marked the nasal bones of the rhinos where their horns had been hacked off. The older skulls, bleached white by the sun and washed clean by rain, seemed more bereft of life than those still covered patchily with dark, sun-dried flesh. All seemed to grimace more painfully than any other skulls I'd seen.

It struck me suddenly that Coletrane relished this shed full of death; it was his natural habitat. Behind his kindliness there lurked the ancient imperative of the implacable hunter. I glanced at Eva. Her eyes were bright with the kind of joy I'd seen before only when we'd made love. Coletrane had an absentminded smile on his face.

I turned to him. 'All poached?'

He nodded. 'Every one. We've got a small anti-poaching team, but the poachers are armed with AK 47 assault rifles so our chaps with their old three-oh-threes are simply outgunned.' He closed the door.

'Better get you chaps settled in your tent,' he said, and called out loudly to his camp staff in vernacular. Soon we were surrounded by smiling blacks to whom we were introduced one by one. We shook hands. They carried our luggage away.

'Your tent's over there, by that cordyla tree,' said Coletrane.

'That's wonderful, Daddy, thank you,' said Eva. 'Isn't this a wonderful camp?' she said to me.

'Wonderful, wonderful,' I answered. I turned to Coletrane. 'What're you going to do about the elephant?'

'Not sure yet. I'm going to have a chat with the villagers who came down to report it, see what they have to say. Long walk . . .'

'Are you going to shoot it?'

'Don't know yet. May have to if he's in pain.'

'Can't you just dart him?'

'Have you ever darted an elephant?'

'No; but –'

'It's not as easy at it looks on the films. We do have a Cap-Chur rifle and plenty of M-99; but we'd have to operate and for that we'd need a vet and that I fear we don't have. Don't want to kill him. Depends how sick he is. Don't want to.'

I looked straight into his charming blue eyes. 'Don't you?'

He stared back at me. 'No,' he said with the smallest smile. 'I've shot enough. Don't need to shoot another.'

'Are there a lot of elephants here?'

'Plenty. But not dangerous ones. So don't get a fright tonight when the elephants come into camp; they're after the cordyla fruit, not you.'

'Not me,' I said with a smile.

He smiled back. 'Not yet, old boy, not yet ...' He walked away, calling to his camp staff: 'Jumaaaa! Muemaaaa! ...'

'Bwanaaa!' I heard them chorus in reply.

I turned to Eva. 'Why do you call him Daddy?'

She looked at me in silence for a moment. Then, with a shrug and a look of indifference she said, 'He's my father. Why shouldn't I?'

THREE

Dawn was still a long time off when I woke. My mouth was gin-dried and my head ached. Another hangover. The tide was going out, I could tell from the muffled sound of the waves on the shore. I stretched, got up, made coffee and stood on the porch sipping it, shivering in the chill, watching the sloppy ebb-tide waves drag the flotsam of the storm back into the forgiving sea: wrack, sea-grape, crayfish shells, black mussels, dead fish, old worn logs and the unromantic jetsam of the Taiwanese trawlers that plundered the coast: neatly-knotted condoms, plastic buoys, shampoo bottles and poly-propylene line. The storm rain had left the air cold but the clouds were gone and the wind had swung back to the south east. Good weather.

I checked on Ludwig who looked better than before, gave him his tablets and a dish of warm milk and set off down the beach on my long-delayed fitness run. I don't enjoy it but you can't scuba in the frigid Cape waters if you're unfit, and there was a church on the next beach at Bakoven that I wanted to visit. It was a small corrugated iron and wood chapel that had been built almost a century ago in memory of the sailors who'd gone down on a small freighter in one of those bad northwesters that spring up so quickly in winter. I liked it. I sometimes went to the little church when it was empty to light a candle for the people I love who have gone; why, I don't know. I have no faith in this tinkering with the Absolute.

That morning I lit no candle nor was I good at praying. But I did kneel, briefly, and tried to explain why I was such a failure, and genuflected uncomfortably. Then I stole out of the church and ran home as the sun rose behind the mountains and lit up the sea.

Mandy telephoned at nine-thirty to say she had to visit a friend who was sick with tick-bite fever contracted while 'doing naughty things with her boyfriend on a rug', up on the slopes amongst the pines in the Glen above Camps Bay. I asked how old the friend was, and she told me fourteen, but she looks much older. When I asked the age of the boyfriend I was astounded when told he was twenty nine, but Mandy found this unsurprising.

'I can come and visit you tonight, if you like, but you'll have to bring me home, I'm not allowed to walk alone at night.'

'That'll be fine,' I said. 'But no nonsense.'

'Nonsense?' she said with a little giggle, and rang off.

I pottered about cleaning and vacuuming. I long ago gave up the luxury of a maid; the intrusions on my privacy were too acute and I enjoyed the mindless discipline of housework. Mandy was much in my mind. What a strange little girl. She clearly wanted more than the fumbling orgasms of teenage-hood, was on the brink of making her sacrifice to the goddess Hymen, and if it wasn't me, I told myself, it would probably be some pimply gangly twit in his twenties, or the sweaty-palmed father of one of her friends.

I finished my housework and walked along the empty early-morning beach to the rocky point with my wetsuit and goggles and a snorkel and collected two dozen oysters from the unplundered virgin bed I'd been saving for a special occasion.

★

She came at seven-thirty, dressed in jeans and a blue jersey, materializing out of the warm twilight like a small blond sprite. She hugged me tightly and I saw that she'd brought a black leather overnight bag.

'And the bag?' I asked.

'You'll see. I've got a present for you later.' She stared critically at my face. 'Your beard's coming on nicely. What's for supper?'

'Steak tartare?'

'Yummy. I told all my friends about your steak tartare, but they all say it sounds disgusting. I love it. Can I have some wine please?'

'White?'

'Red?'

'Red's very heavy.'

'Mummy always lets me have red.'

'Very well, red it shall be. But not just yet. I've got a surprise for you first . . .'

'What?' She was all sparkling eyes and undisguised delight.

'You'll see.'

I was slightly appalled by the pleasure she brought me. It was as though we were old lovers. Perhaps it was the evening, the thick still air hanging hot all around, the distant luminous light of dusk. I laid a thick white linen cloth on the table on the porch, put out my decent silver, lit candles and opened a bottle of dark red wine full of the taste of blood and honey and a flinty ice-cold Graves for the oysters.

She'd never eaten oysters and regarded them with distaste.

'They look awful,' she said.

'Nonsense. They're beautiful. And you of all people should enjoy them. They taste of the sea. The first one is the most difficult; after that it's easy. Just add a little tabasco, a little lemon, fork it up, pop it in your mouth, chew it, take a bite of brown bread and a sip of wine and that's it.' She did so and her face lit up with amazement and pleasure.

'They taste wonderful!'

'I told you so.'

'They taste the way it feels to swim,' she said. 'But I don't like the tabasco, it gets in the way of the taste.'

I nodded, pleased. 'I agree. Just lemon.' She tucked in, making little feral sounds of delight. I felt a paternal pride watching her. She drank her wine with real pleasure, exclaiming over the dry stony taste. I told her about the gravel soil where the vines grow, how they struggle in the aridity, how the unique granite taste is compressed into the grapes and miraculously preserved in the wine. She listened with interest, asked acute questions and smiled at my silly jokes. Her eyes were bright in the candle light and she looked very beautiful. She would break many hearts in years to come.

★

After the steak tartare I gave her meringue chantilly which she ate slowly and thoughtfully. Her mood had changed and I felt a little dismayed. Had the wine made her maudlin?

I asked her.

'I've never had so much fun in my life,' she replied slowly. 'I feel that I've known you forever. You know so much.'

'Not really,' I said. 'It's just that I'm so much older than you, I've seen more, learnt more.'

She sighed. 'But that's what I mean. All the boys I know are so silly compared to you. They don't know anything. They're so stupid. Not like you ...'

'That's not their fault,' I said gently. 'And nothing can come of this, Mandy. It's totally impractical.'

'Who says everything has to be practical?' she replied quickly. 'I really love you.'

'Mandy, Mandy. I'm fond of you too, but it can't work.'

'Can we be friends for ever, then?'

'For ever,' I said.

She brightened. 'Good. Now I'm going to give you your present.' She disappeared inside, humming to herself.

She re-appeared on the porch wearing her school uniform: blazer, white shirt, tie, grey gymslip, white ankle socks and sandals. She looked all of ten years old. I stared at her.

'I want you to see something,' she said. 'Come and sit in the sitting room ...' She led me by the hand to an armchair she'd positioned so that I could see into my bedroom. She walked into the bedroom, turned on a light and, ignoring me entirely, began to undress. When she had stripped to her white school bra and sensible white cotton panties, she began to dress in a short black satin skirt of my ex-wife's. She bent, slid off her panties beneath the skirt and put on a black satin g-string. Turning her back, she unclipped the white bra, slipped on a red silk blouse and buttoned it. Then she drew on stockings, her pale legs somehow defenceless, fragile against the black nylon. She turned to Eva's dressing table and put on a pair of golden hoop earrings, eyeliner and lipstick, and I thought of the courtesans of ancient Egypt who'd reddened their lips with sweet dye to ward off evil spirits. Finally she sipped on the pair of high black patent shoes she'd brought before.

She turned to face me, fixed my eyes with hers and walked to me and put her arms around me and hugged me close and said, 'I know you liked that.'

I watched her glittering eyes.

'Do you understand now?'

'Yes,' I said. 'I think so.'

She smiled at me. 'Shall we go outside and finish our wine?'

'Yes,' I said and followed her little swinging rump out onto the porch. We drank our wine in silence and listened to the sea.

After a little while she said, 'Are you feeling sad?'

'No. Why?'

'I can't see you in the dark and I know you get sad sometimes.'

'I'm a natural melancholic,' I said.

'A what?'

'I get sad easily.'

'Is it your wife?'

'Sometimes. Sometimes not.'

'Will you tell me all about it one day?'

Would I. Would I? Remembering what happened in central Africa, I doubted that I'd ever tell anyone.

FOUR

The first night we slept in Coletrane's camp the elephants came, just as he'd predicted. I was woken by the loud crack of a breaking branch. I lay in the dark and listened happily then got up and opened the tent flap. Full moonlight lit the bush. Two young bull elephants were ten paces away under the cordyla tree, snuffling with their trunks along the ground, searching for fruit. The rest of the herd had spread out through the mopane. Some had bent down saplings with their trunks until the trees broke with a crack; they browsed on the fresh green leaves. I sat and watched them until dawn came, when they rumbled deep in their stomachs and at some unheard signal gathered together in the pale mopane and disappeared in their silent way.

Breakfast was served in the open-sided pole-and-thatch structure that Eva called a chitenje. The waiters came and went in silence, bringing paw-paw and ripe mangoes, eggs and bacon, toast and tea. One of them placed a catapult and some stones beside Coletrane's plate. He caught my glance.

'Monkeys,' he said briefly. 'Got to keep them under control.'

'Ah,' I said innocently. 'I thought it might have been for the elephants I saw last night.' He gave me a baleful blue-eyed look, then said, 'What elephants?'

I told him about the elephants and asked about their rumbles.

'Communication. Sub-audio for us, most of the time. Infrasound, I think the boffins call it. Damned interesting actually. They keep up that purring noise all the time; call each other and all sorts of things. Warning.'

'And the herd last night? What would they have been?'

'Oh, cows and calves, young bulls, juveniles. Big bulls leave the herd, only join up for mating, so forth. Eating the cordylas?'

'Yes, and mopane.'

'Bastards are hammering the mopane here, eating themselves out of house and home just the way they did back in the sixties. Had to cull them then; may have to cull them again.'

'How many did you shoot?'

'One thousand four hundred and sixty four over a four year period, starting in 'sixty-five.'

'Quite a lot.'

'Not enough. Funny thing, we dumped all the bones not far from here in the mopane. Didn't see a jumbo in there for years, and they love the mopane. Then one day I was in there with Kalilombe, spooring a big leopard in the soft sand and there was a bloody great tusker in there, teeth like telephone poles, just standing there, dead quiet, with an elephant femur in his trunk, just holding it.'

'Good lord.'

'Yes. Damn strange. Damn strange. Seen it often, don't understand it at all. Mind you, the old hunters' books are full of gumph about elephants and death. Jumbos detouring for miles through the bush to visit skeletons of dead elephants, so forth. Always bury a hunter they've killed. Always with branches, sort of elephant burial service. Never seen it, heard about it . . . Damn strange.'

'What's happened to that big bull the poachers wounded?' asked Eva.

'Kalilombe's going off to sort that out tomorrow.' He glanced at me, spread apricot jam thickly on his toast. No butter. I think he regarded butter as an extravagance or a sign of moral weakness. Copying him, I spread jam thinly on my toast, scorned butter. You've got to live tough in the tropics.

'Paul, don't know if it's your sort of thing, but I thought you might like to go along with Kalilombe. See the bush?'

'I'd like that very much,' I said, feeling guilty about mocking him when he was really a rather generous man. 'But surely we'll be in the way?'

'We?' said Eva. 'I'm not going with you. I'm staying here in camp with Daddy.'

'You're not going either, then?' I said to Coletrane.

'No need. Kalilombe'll sort it all out. He's very good. Kalilombe means chameleon in the vernacular. Good name for a tracker. Looks everywhere, sees everything.'

'I'd like to go very much,' I said. 'Why does he look so sad?'

He glanced at me with raised eyebrows. 'You noticed something?'

'Yes.'

'His wife was taken by a croc down by the river when fetching water a couple of weeks ago.'

'Good God, no!' said Eva in horror. Coletrane nodded.

'Nasty business. Seems he really loved her. Trouble is, he can't talk about it, come to terms with it.'

'Should he be able to?' I asked.

He glanced at me, broke another piece of toast. 'Why not? Shouldn't mope ...'

I shrugged, stared at him.

'Perhaps you're right,' he said.

'Take no notice of him, Daddy,' said Eva. 'He says things sometimes just to be provocative.'

Coletrane smiled politely and said, 'Anyway, I thought it would do him good to get away and if you'd like to go along, so much the better. Give him someone to look after.'

'When do we leave?'

'Tomorrow morning early. Kalilombe's driven into Pamwala for supplies. And we've got guests for dinner tonight.'

'Oh, who?' asked Eva. 'Anyone I know?'

'Yes; Jimmy and Diana Cheveley, d'you remember them?'

'Oh, God no! I mean, yes of course I remember them! Is she still such a bitch?'

'Yes.'

'Oh, God, no! And is he still drinking himself to death?'

'Yes, I'm afraid so.'

'They're dreadful, Daddy. Diana'll just get drunk and abusive. She's awful. What on earth did you ask them to dinner for?'

'I quite like them, actually,' he said mildly. 'You shouldn't be so critical, Eva.' He turned to me. 'She was always very critical, even as a tiny thing.'

'She hasn't changed,' I said drily.

'Yes, but why did you ask them to dinner?' persisted Eva. 'You knew I'd be here, and I wanted to have some time alone with you, you know that.' She pouted sulkily.

'I'm sorry my darling,' said Coletrane. 'They arrived in camp late last night on their way back from Chinjuzu up on the escarpment. It's a long haul without a stop'. He glanced at his watch. 'Too early for them for breakfast, never get up till noon,' he said with faint disapproval.

'Are they staying long?' asked Eva, still with a hint of a pout.

'No; they'll be gone tomorrow.'

'Oh, goody! So we'll have the camp to ourselves?'

'Totally.'

'You won't even have me here to pester you,' I said. They both stared at me as if I'd crawled out from under a rock.

FIVE

Despite Eva's moods, dinner was splendid. It was served by
the camp servants in the chitenje which was lit by hissing
Petromax lanterns. Insects dinked against the lamp glasses.
The long table was laid with a gay red and white checked
tablecloth and the servants were dressed in khaki trousers and
smart white jackets but everything seemed too colonial to be
real. Coletrane clearly upheld the standards of the golden age
of safari in the 'thirties, and in the older men's conversations
I discerned an acute longing for a past when both blacks and
women knew their place in the scheme of things and didn't
answer back. I found them quaint. They were a museum of
'thirties affectations and dotty verbal mannerisms. I couldn't
make myself dislike them.

Guests drifted in slowly, helped themselves to drinks and
chatted, the men dressed in khaki longs, neat bushjackets and
cravats, the women in bright summer evening dresses. Eva,
braless, looked lovely in a low-cut scarlet evening dress in a
silky clinging knit. The evening was hot and humid but the
moon was not yet up and the surrounding bush was dark and
quiet.

There were eleven of us: Dickie and Eva and me, Jimmy and
Diana Cheveley; Margot and 'Yobbo' de Vere who were old
friends of Dickie's, also just passing through; another old
hunting friend of Dickie's, Bob Tincker-Smith, known as
'Bobs', a quiet inward man with whispy white hair and a
grave, melancholic expression on his face and a way of
looking at people with great sadness down his bony patrician
nose; a dark saturnine young man invited by Coletrane, a
professional hunter whose name I didn't catch, who looked at
Eva's breasts all evening as though he'd like to shoot them

and hang them on his wall; and two bearded blond men with sunburnt faces who were doing research into something called pistia stratiotes which turned out to be a river weed no animal would eat. This seemed an exercise in futility to me and I said so, only to be greeted with the arrogant pitying look some bush people reserve for uninformed townies. There was casual discussion about the fact that Coletrane's camp was sited in the caldera of an extinct volcano. I pondered this, wondering if molten rock still seethed below us, waiting patiently for its time to come round again.

While we dressed for dinner, Eva had given me a jaundiced view of Diana Cheveley. Childhood memories. She was an 'awful woman.' Eva remembered Diana wearing 'beautifully cut white jodhs one size too small.' She was 'always hanging around Daddy'; and it seemed she'd violated some obscure unspoken code by carrying a small pearl-handled revolver with which she unerringly shot snakes which threatened her pony when she rode the grasslands at dawn. And her lipstick was always 'too red.' She also 'hated everyone' and got disgustingly drunk and 'insulted people.' I decided to reserve judgement. To me, Diana Cheveley was very beautiful, despite her age and the pixie-like look resulting from one facelift too many. She had a long wild mane of grey-streaked auburn hair, and with careful makeup passed for forty five, although I'm certain she was over sixty.

She had very lovely hands, which she used slowly and with grace, and a voice abraded by gin and cigarettes. She toyed with her food. She wore a barbaric-looking silver cross on a fine chain about her neck. Her husband Jimmy, a thin sallow man who chain-smoked from a pack of thirty, had a racking cough that sucked in his concave chest. He wore Clark's desert boots without socks and his head was perched on a neck as wrinkled and stringy as that of a tortoise. He and Coletrane had been in the Game Department together.

Margot and Yobbo were about fifty and had been married for a year. Yobbo talked with a pronounced Yorkshire accent but looked like a Spanish nobleman painted by El Greco. He had dark cruel eyes and a Shakespearean beard and looked as if he belonged on the poop deck of a galleon wearing galligaskins and a rapier. He was apparently from an excessively noble but impoverished family, and had been banished to an ordinary day school when his contemporaries had all been at Eton, hence his accent and nickname. A third son, on leaving school he was immediately despatched to the Colonies to seek work. Margot was a dreamy ex-beauty who talked wistfully about 'the old days' in Kenya where she'd grown up. I had the feeling that she was a fragile creature. Yobbo's concern for her was quite touching: he fetched her 'heart tablets' from their tent, cautioned her about drinking too much red wine, spoke knowledgeably about her neurasthenia.

The buffalo-tail soup was followed by roast guinea-fowl in mango sauce. Quantities of Portugese wine were drunk by all except Bobs and Dickie, both of whom drank neat whisky throughout. When the roast buffalo fillet was served Diana Cheveley began to tease Dickie and Bobs. I was fascinated. Eva looked disapproving. Bobs looked more melancholic than ever and Dickie watched her with his chilly obsidian stare. She began with the bearded blond researchers, whom she had christened Tweedledum and Tweedledee.

Playing with the stem of her wine glass, she had for some while listened with a look of profound boredom to a discourse on calibres suitable for killing elephant, conducted with soporific relentlessness by Tweedledum and Tweedledee.

'The four-seventy,' said Tweedledum. 'Beautiful calibre.' He enumerated on his fingers. 'Excellent penetration, excellent muzzle velocity, excellent knock-down power.'

'Ballistically identical to the four-five-eight,' explained Tweedledee helpfully.

'Although the four-five-eight is noted for some spectacular bullet failures,' warned Teedledum. 'I saw a solid that riveted and broke up on an elephant skull during a cull in Kruger. Bad performance.'

'I personally like the old four-sixteen Rigby,' countered the other.

'Tremendous penetration. Bullet weighs –'

'– four hundred and ten grains, my God, you men are boring,' said Diana. A shocked silence fell. Margot giggled. 'Don't tell me they're talking about elephant turds again,' she said.

'No; if only they were. No, they're going on and on and on about rifle calibres. I swear I could write a book about elephant rifles.' She turned to the two men. 'Why are all you men so infinitely convinced of your own brilliance?' She turned back to the table. 'I have lived in Africa for –'

'– Centuries!' said Margot, and tinkled her crystalline laugh.

'Don't be a bitch, Margot,' said Diana. 'I have lived in Africa for ages, and during every dinner over the years, from Marsabit to Mangoche, I have been treated to a remarkably dull lecture on bullets and how to kill large animals. Don't you men ever think about anything else?'

'The elephant problem is part of Africa,' said Tweedledum stiffly.

'I know so much about bloody elephants I should pro'bly have a trunk,' snapped Diana. She turned to me. 'They're so smug, all of them. Convinced they're somehow better than everyone else because they know the difference between a coucal and a cuckooshrike!'

'What's a coucal?' I asked innocently and saw a pitying glance pass between Tweedledum and Tweedledee.

'You see?' said Margot. 'You see? Smug. Too stupid for self-examination, too.' She shook her head at them. 'You'd think the bush would've taught them humility, above all, but no; they're as bad as the idiots in the city they affect to despise so much.'

'You bunny-huggers just don't understand hunting,' said the young professional hunter, dragging his eyes away from Eva's bust for a second. His eyes were hooded and narrowed by alcohol.

'I'm not talking about hunting,' said Diana. 'I happen to have a professional hunter's license and I expect I've shot more poor bloody elephants than you've even seen.'

I watched them all, remembered it all: the hot night and the whine of the mosquitoes, the beetles dive-bombing the gas-lamps, the servants coming and going in silence, the abandoned filigree wings of the flying ants who coupled shamelessly end-to-end amongst the breadcrumbs, and the men's studied indifference because it was only a woman talking. Women were bad news in the bush. Africa was full of stories about 'kali memsahibs' who weren't tough enough for the tropics.

'No; what I'm talking about,' continued Diana, 'is vanity. All you bloody men are so berluddy self-conscious about your image. Not at all the sort of self-effacing chaps you'd expect and they all pretend to be. And they're all ex military men, too, with all that implies.' She sipped her wine and looked at me.

'What does it imply?' I asked.

'Well, that's easy; in my day they were nice, dull unimaginative men. You know. Don't pretend to be so stupid, it doesn't suit you.'

'He always does that, it's infuriating,' said Eva.

Diana ignored her. 'Salt of the earth,' she added. 'But awful lovers, all the same. All of them. Clumsy.'

'Clumsy?' I said, amazed. The men I'd met all looked perfectly well-coordinated.

'Rubbish,' said the dark young hunter, and smiled at Eva. She smiled back, the bitch.

'Well, unsubtle then. They'd sort of hang around when one's husband was off on safari, knocking the dottle out of their pipes all over the hollyhocks, mooning about at drinks time with silly little fixed grins on their faces like fox terriers after a bitch. Sooner or later some poor woman gave in – God knows why, they all had pink knees: I suppose out of pity rather than lust – and went to bed with one of them.'

'Usually you,' said Yobbo.

'And out of loneliness,' Diana continued. 'And don't be rude to me Yobbo or I'll tell everyone why your family really sent you to Africa. I mean, our husbands seemed more interested in the company of other men than they did in us. Or finding out what crocodiles ate, which in itself was pretty stupid since they clearly ate the locals. Every croc Jimmy ever shot had about twenty brass bracelets in its stomach and the clearest memory I have of my first husband is him up to his knees in intestines, disembowelling a hippo. He never could explain why. Frankly, there was more fun to be had riding a camel than going to bed with one of those men. But they were terribly sincere,' she added.

'Why did you, then?' I asked.

'They were all we had! And we'd been sort of taught that we ought to like those sort of men because they were The Empire Builders.'

'Oh, rot!' said Yobbo.

Margot giggled. 'It's true, Yobbo.'

'It's absolutely true,' said Diana. 'Even when I was young – which wasn't that long ago, despite what Margot says – the whole idea of Empire was still terribly strong. And these were the men we'd grown up with.'

'I refuse to believe I'm vain,' said Yobbo.

'You're all vain,' retorted Diana.

'In what way?' asked Dickie.

'Yes,' I said. 'How?'

'Well, they all had a silly competition once, something about eccentric hats. The chap with the nastiest hat won truly enormous respect, you see. Or they'd compete to see how austere they could be. They'd go without water for ages, until their kidneys packed in. I remember Dickie going without water for days up in the desert. He was in a mission hospital for a week. Stupid. Little boys.'

'Saved her life once,' said Bobs from the shadows. 'She always forgets that. Got herself lost.'

'You forget: I got lost looking for my second husband –'

'Third,' interjected Margot.

'– oh, all right, third; because the silly bastard ran out of water Being Austere,' said Diana briskly. 'Jimmy's the same. Won't wear socks, hates shoelaces. Silly, you see. Babies. Gives people something to say about them because they're all so deadly dull. Even good old Bobs is the same; camp full of Persian carpets; and that dull stick over there, the one who can't keep his eyes off Eva, he's stopped wearing socks as well, wears bandanas instead. Can't read, hardly speak, most of them; shave every day of course, but that's not enough to build a marriage on, is it?'

'I suppose not,' I said quickly.

'Of course it's not.'

'Do shut up about the socks,' said Dickie plaintively.

'Course, Dickie's better than most,' said Diana judiciously. 'And good old Bobs. Thinks a bit now and again, does Bobs. But he's like Dickie: they only do it because their wives left them. Dickie's wife left him for one of his hunting clients. Poor Dickie, disturbed his whole universe.'

'Leave Daddy alone,' said Eva. 'And anyway, mother was a cow to do that.'

'Sorry, darling; but he was rather cut up, wasn't he? Couldn't understand it, it was all supposed to happen the other way round, you see. Great White Hunter, strong silent type, eyes used to vast distances, man who'd Plumbed the Secrets Only Africa Can Teach, manly, sensitive-yet-strong, all that.'

'Diana, do shut up,' said Cheveley.

'Course, fact that the client was a millionaire must've had something to do with it,' she mused. 'Don't you think, Dickie?'

'You're a bitch, Diana,' said Coletrane quietly. 'And you're drunk.'

He turned and bellowed into the darkness: 'Jumaaaa!'

'Bwanaaaaaa!' came the reply.

'Pudding!' shouted Coletrane.

Margot smiled sweetly. 'Dickie always loved his pudding, such a sweet tooth,' she said. 'Even when he was a little boy; he was enormously fat, you know. His mummy told me!'

Diana seemed to calm down when the fresh fruit salad and tinned cream was served, and conversation became more general. But by the time the savoury made from guinea-fowl and francolin liver arrived at table, Tweedledum and Tweedledee had forgotten their chastisement and were remorselessly boring Diana again, this time about trees.

Bobs wandered past on his way to replenish his whisky from the drinks tray and stopped to listen, eyes moving from one sunburnt bearded face to the other with a look of profound sorrow.

'You have the bastard baobab here, I saw one just up the road,' said Tweedledum.

'Yes. Sterculia africana. Part of the Star Chestnut family, actually,' said the other.

'To name is not to know,' said Bobs suddenly, very softly but with great intensity. 'To name is not to know. Always remember that.' Then he turned away to replenish his drink. This seemed finally to stop the bearded twins, and they ate their cheese and passed the port in numbed silence.

Diana spoke to me: 'What do you think of this cheese?'

'It's very good, don't you think? Like Bel Paese.'

'Do you really think so? Please, you must tell Jimminy, he'll be so delighted. He made it and it's his first attempt.'

'Of course I will. Did you say Jimminy?'

'Yes, my nickname for him because he looks so like a cricket doesn't he?' It was impossible for me to agree with that so I simply smiled. She twinkled at me and I felt the impact of her violet eyes and a personality so adept at talking trivia that she revealed herself only by accident. I found myself interested in her.

'Your cross is very unusual,' I said.

'Yes. Do you like it?'

'Very much.'

'It's Tuareg, not really a Christian cross at all. It's called the Chameleon's Eye,' she added, and pointed to an engraved motif: two crossed lines with a dot in each of the right-angles thus formed. 'See? That's the Chameleon's Eye. It confers second sight on the wearer, and great wisdom. It was given me by an old witch doctor up in Somalia.'

'It's very lovely. Does it work?'

She twinkled at me, but did not answer. 'How did you meet Eva?' she asked.

'I'm a photographer,' I answered, 'and Eva was modelling. We met on a shoot and it sort of happened from there.'

'She's exquisite, isn't she?'

'Oh yes. Wonderful bones.'

'Beauty like that can be so dangerous, you know,' she said musingly, intent on slicing a thin sliver of Jimminy's cheese. 'It tempts a girl to rely on that alone to get through her life. Do you know what I mean?'

I nodded.

'And she was always Daddy's favourite girl, you know. Even as a little thing she learnt so early that being all blond and girlish was the best way to Daddy's heart. And she wanted so much for him to love her only, you know. Because he was such a hero, in Africa. Did you know that? No? Well, he was; he was a very good hunter when being a Great White Hunter was rather like being an astronaut or something. Him and Bobs, though Bobs was always a little too much of a mystic to be really glamorous. He saw the bush differently, as if it were a sort of proving ground for souls. That interests you, does it?' she said with a tiny smile.

'Yes, I like that ... idea.'

'Perhaps we should go together with Bobs to watch the moonrise, then,' she said slowly, watching me. 'He and I always go together, if we meet and it's full moon. Would you like to?'

'Very much. Thank you.'

'We'll drive a little way to a place I know,' she said. 'It's not far. The moon won't be as good as a few nights back, but it'll still be worth seeing.' Then: 'Look at her. Isn't she lovely ...'

Eva was laughing at something her father had said, and he and the young hunter were watching her with undisguised delight. I noticed that Yobbo was watching the young hunter with a look of quiet appraisal. His eyes strayed down the open shirtfront, lingered on the dark pelt of chest hair and I understood why his family had packed him off to Africa.

'Yeees,' said Diana, watching Eva. 'You know, girls who love their daddies that much never love any other man properly. I didn't. My father seemed such a complete man. He was brave and gentle and strong and sensitive and a bit of a pirate, I thought. And no man I met seemed to me to measure up. They defined themselves by their jobs, somehow. They were accountants, or brokers or something; they weren't simply men. Their centres were soft. They were diminished people. And girls like me always marry the wrong men, on purpose. Men who are patently no threat to the sacred relationship they have with their daddies.' Her bright eyes observed me carefully for my reaction.

'Are you warning me?'

She twinkled. 'You don't need a warning, do you?'

'I don't know,' I said. 'Do I?'

'And if they do involve themselves with men who are a true threat,' she said, ignoring my question, 'they chip away at that love until it crumbles.' Watching me very carefully now, she went on: 'You see, they want a strong man, a strong man, who will love them completely, who will kill the image they have of their fathers; because the daddy they love is not real daddy but a sort of mythical dream-creature, a sort of mythical monster that only a hero can kill. Their daddies hold them prisoner. Daddies are dragons who tie us up in their castles and kill off our suitors ...' She laughed delightedly to herself at that. 'So when they find a really strong man ... After all, the holy of holies is reserved for daddy alone, so every act of love is a betrayal, every orgasm a treason. Does this bore you? All this amateur psychoanalysis?'

'Not at all. But should I be monopolising you? Aren't we being rude?'

'No. No one cares what I do any more.'

'Very well. But why are you telling me all this?'

She stared at me for a little while, then said, 'Perhaps I am warning you. You see, if these women find a really strong man, they set about breaking him. And destroying the love to prove to their tyrant daddies that they're not betraying that ... sacred bond. Am I making sense?'

'Of course.'

'To you?'

'Perhaps,' I smiled.

She nodded, then went on vaguely, 'I was in Paris once, when I was about twenty one and I was living a silly life; drinking too much, gambling too much at Le Touquet. And I hadn't seen my daddy for ages. So I cut my wrists. Of course, I didn't know why, then; I told everyone it was weltschmerz and angst. But it wasn't. I wanted my daddy to come and fetch me back to Africa.'

'And did he?'

She looked at me pityingly. 'What a silly question. Of course he did.'

'And then?'

She shrugged, a gesture so slight and expressive it was not Anglo Saxon. 'We were happy together for a time.' She smiled at me.

'Was your father a handsome man?'

'Yes ...' said Diana. 'Very like Dickie. Dickie reminded me so much of my father, when he was young and I was a teenage girl. Dickie was so devastatingly handsome when he was young. Similar type to you, physically, as a matter of fact, except you're not at all handsome because you've got that nose like a potato. He was very dark and cruel-looking, but so gentle women gave in out of gratitude.

'I did, anyway. And then of course he wrote all those books about hunting and animals and conservation and innumerable other things that made all the husbands he'd cuckolded forgive him because he said so beautifully in his books what they'd oft thought but ne'er so well expressed. Eva utterly adores him, you know. Women love heroes.'

'Yes,' I said wryly. 'She does that.'

'You sounded so Kentish then, your accent crept in. Are you from Kent?'

'Yes, near Bredgar.'

'Oh, I know Bredgar, such a tiny sweet village, full of the most wicked people. My father always said it was a gypsey village, which he rather approved of, since he was something of a gypsey, in spirit, himself. He came to Africa so long ago it's indecent, and lived here in a way he wouldn't've been able to in England.'

Bobs came past on his way to the drinks tray for another whisky. Diana caught his sleeve and said: 'Paul's coming to watch the moon with us.'

He looked at me. 'He is, is he?' he murmured with the faintest glimmer of interest. 'Good. We'll go in about an hour. What about Eva? Will she come?'

'I doubt it,' said Diana. 'She's got Dickie instead.'

'Yes ...' said Bobs with a minute desiccated smile. 'She's always had Dickie instead.'

The party broke up shortly after. I told Eva and Dickie that I was going to watch the moonrise with Bobs and Diana. Dickie looked intrigued. Eva declined. 'I'll stay and have a nightcap with Daddy and Justin.'

'Who's Justin?' I asked.

'Oh, that young guy, the hunter, you know,' she said casually. 'He's gone for a pee.'

'The twit?' I said, hoping he'd get bitten by a mamba.

'He's not a twit,' she protested. 'He's like Daddy, he loves Africa.'

'Does he?' I said. 'Or does he like the idea of it? Society hunter?'

'Don't be absurd, he loves Africa. You wouldn't understand.'

'No? Perhaps you mean he's prepared to humour you and your fantasies.'

'All I said is he's not a twit.'

'He is a bit,' said Coletrane. 'But he's young still and he's quite a good hunter.'

He smiled at me and I looked into those chilly blue eyes that crinkled so charmingly at the corners to put one off the spoor of his true nature and I knew instantly and without doubt why Justin was in camp and why I was being sent off into the bundu.

'I still think he's a twit,' I said.

'Not a bit,' said Eva. 'He's young still.'

'Eva likes him because he's pretty,' I said. 'She adores beautiful men. It was one of the first things she ever told me.'

'Yes,' said Coletrane. 'She was always like that.' He chuckled indulgently.

'What time are you leaving in the morning?' Eva asked.

'Early,' said Coletrane. 'You should be on your way just before sunup, if you can. I've sent the safari ahead in one of the Land Rovers. I thought you'd like to walk with Kalilombe. Like the old days. He's very good, you'll be quite safe. The boys'll have your camp pitched by the time you get in in the evening, fire going, tent up, bwana's chair ready, drinks waiting.'

'Why do you call them boys?' I asked.

'Nothing derogatory,' he said. 'Comes from the old ex-Indian Army chaps; in India there was a servant cast called "Bhoi"; Bee Aitch Oh Aye. No reference to age.'

'And ghirl was another, I suppose?'

'What?'

'Ghirl with an aitch.'

He looked at me with his predator's eyes and said nothing.

Justin walked up, unsteadily but with determination in every assured step. He was wearing faded blue jeans, cowboy boots and an old starched white dress shirt with a pique front, open at the neck. The whole effect appeared very casual yet it was contrived with great care. He smiled boyishly at me and I looked him straight in the eye to see what he was really like. He avoided my eyes and grinned at Eva instead. He was nearly as tall as me, but younger, trimmer and tauter. There was no air of danger about him as there was about Coletrane, but he had long lashes and treacle-black eyes and hair as dark as a blackbird's wing. His teeth were very white.

'What about that nightcap?' he said, grinning at Eva.

'Help yourself,' said Coletrane with a smile.

I walked away.

SIX

It was almost midnight when we met at the Land Rover, Diana, Bobs and I. Diana was still in her evening dress but she'd changed her patent leather evening shoes for a pair of plimsolls.

'I'll drive,' she said. 'We can all fit in the front.' We squeezed together, Bobs in the middle. 'I brought you a cigar,' he said to Diana. 'Quite nice. Hoyo ... You've always liked Hoyo, haven't you?' He handed it to her. He offered one to me, which I accepted out of politeness. It struck me that they'd been lovers at some stage and I sensed I was intruding on some private ritual. We drove in silence for a time and I realised that they'd never before asked anyone to join them on their visits to the full moon. I felt uncomfortable but slightly flattered, as if they knew something about me I didn't yet know myself. Diana drove along a rutted track. Birds, resting in the warm dust, took to panic flight as we approached, pale and filmy-winged in the light of our headlamps. 'What birds are those?'

'Pennant-winged nightjars,' answered Bobs. 'In mating plumage. See those long wings? Drives their womenfolk wild with desire.'

'They're very beautiful.'

'So you're off on safari tomorrow?'

'Yes.'

'I had a word with Kalilombe when he got back with your supplies. Apparently the tusker you're after has moved a bit further north, across the Red Plain, into the riverine bush on the far side of the Imzinduzu. Killed two more tribesmen on the way.'

'The Red Plain? What an odd name.'

'Yes; actually, it can be translated two ways. The old-timers call it that, but the locals translate it as the Plain of Darkness. Evidently they attach some spiritual significance to it, but I've never been able to find out exactly what. They're rather reticent.'

'Here we are,' said Diana and parked under a tall thorn tree. I could just see the straggly branches outlined against the stars.

'You lead,' she said to Bobs, who'd produced a rifle from somewhere. I heard him work the bolt.

'What calibre's that?' I asked.

'Four-oh-four. Old Cogswell and Harrison. Sorry about the drama, but we can't be too careful. Probably won't need it at all but I don't want to get you bitten by a lioness with cubs or anything stupid like that.'

I followed them through the bush. The night was very still. There were no insect sounds, nor sound of any living thing but there was a heady scent of acacia blossom, as though a beautiful woman wearing a great perfume walked invisible beside us in the dark. We entered a stand of high grass, pale in the night, the seed-heads taller than me, the smell hot and dusty. I felt a moment's apprehension: what if there were buffalo lurking, lion, leopards? But nothing leapt out at us. True, there were furtive scurryings, and once something large crashed away through the bush to our left but Bobs didn't even bother to lower the rifle from where he carried it comfortably balanced butt backwards on his shoulder, the barrel gripped just behind the front sight. We came finally to a small cluster of rocks. We climbed to the top and sat, waiting.

I looked up. There were meadows of stars, seas of stars that I'd never seen before. There were stars the colour of snake's blood, stars the colour of bile and chartreuse and irises; stars as pale as ginger ale, that disappeared when I looked directly at them, stars as brittle as ice, as luminous as distant camp-fires. Orion was up, and the Southern Cross, and Vega and Deneb and Altair, making a giant celestial triangle. We seemed to be facing due east, towards a range of stony hills topped with flat-crowned umbrella thorns. The hills of the volcano were all about us.

'Well?' I said.

'Sssh. Watch.'

It started as a faint cigarette-end glow. Then a wild, molten light crept above the rim of the hills. For an instant I thought the volcano had roused itself but then the full moon slid smoothly up out of the darkness behind the hills. Magnified by the heat or the dense tropical air it loomed bigger than any moon I've ever seen. It was the raw yellow of a Van Gogh Arles moon, the chrome orange of pom-pom acacia blossom, an intensity no watercolourist could ever attempt. It was not reflected light; it was savage primeval fire.

The moonlight touched us, and lit up the bush all around. For a moment, stupidly, I expected it to stop and hang there just above the hills but it rose up relentlessly, unstoppable. I was frightened and elated. Then, quickly, it was just a moon again: silver, pale, a cinder. I felt the magic pass.

Bobs and Diana lit cigars, the fragrance sweet in the night.

'Well, what'd'you think?' asked Diana. She drew on her cigar and it glowed like a predator's eye.

I did not immediately answer because I knew that something had changed in me. I was inhabited. It was as if an archaic part of me, long-sleeping, had been woken by the moonlight. It was as if I harboured a god.

'I think you already know,' I said.

'Bobs says Africa's a very old continent,' said Eva, in a faintly mocking voice. 'Don't you Bobs?'

'Sometimes,' said Bobs.

'He says civilization doesn't graft on too well. The gods here are still alive, he says. The people here still have contact with them. Bob's says it's still possible here to conceive of gods who can combat evil, who can respond if you ask for help, don't you Bobs? He says none of the local gods has ever been crucified because these people like their gods too much to kill them.'

Bobs said nothing.

'Problem is,' said Diana, 'they crucify each other instead. Bobs gets a little carried away sometimes,' she said placatingly. 'Don't you, Bobs?

'I expect so,' he said. 'We'd better get back.'

No one spoke until we reached camp. When Diana parked the Land Rover under a towering cordyla, she glanced at Bobs and there was an awkward silence, broken by Bobs who finally said, 'Can you shoot?'

'Yes,' I said, surprised. 'My grandfather taught me. Why?'

'Well, you'd better take this, then,' he said and handed me the old Cogswell and Harrison. It was heavy, and the stock was warm where he'd held it. I tried to give it back but he pressed it into my hands. 'Please take it.'

'What for?'

'Safari. Can't go on safari without a rifle, you may need it,' he said awkwardly. 'If you're not familiar with the action, Kalilombe'll show you, but it's essentially a Mauser. The safety's on, but don't forget there's one up the spout.' He touched my arm lightly and added, 'Go carefully up there, young fellow. Watch and go very carefully.'

To my surprise, Diana leant forward and kissed my cheek. 'And I think you should take this, since you liked it so much.' She reached forward and slipped her chain and Tuareg cross over my head.

'I can't possibly –' I said, but she laid her hand firmly against my mouth.

'Not a word, you silly young man. You can give it back to me some time if you want to. And Bobs is right. Take care . . .'

As one, they turned and disappeared into the night.

'Thanks for showing me the moon,' I called, but they'd gone. Silence. A fishing owl howled upriver.

I showered quickly in the reed and thatch enclosure tucked away in a small clump of monkeythorns. The water smelt of hot cinders. I dried myself and walked the fifty yards through the bush to our tent. The camp staff had lit a Dietz paraffin lantern and placed it by the tent flap. Eva was already asleep. Ma Griffe, her perfume, floated on the hot air. I left the tent flap open. Moonlight shone in.

I pushed over the Mauser safety of the rifle and opened the bolt. The long brass cartridge that Bobs had chambered ejected neatly onto my camp bed. I clicked it down into the magazine well, and depressing all the cartridges against the magazine spring pressure, closed the bolt on the empty chamber. The rifle was old, the blueing worn down to bare silver metal by use. The checkering was almost gone and the stock was badly scratched, though whether by thorns or lion claws or leopard I could not tell; but the action was smooth and the balance was superb. I think it was Homer who said that an unstrung bow is dead but a bow once strung is a living thing. Bobs's rifle felt like that.

I wondered how many times it had saved Bobs's life, how many elephant, buffalo, lion and leopard the rifle had killed. For some reason I could not fathom I felt as if I had held it before, fired it before. But that was clearly fanciful.

I laid the rifle down beside my camp bed and climbed under the covers. I touched the cross around my neck, fingered it in the dark. The moon: that archaic stirring. The moon had been such a strange thing to see, so naked and yellow, seeming to shed flakes of darkness from its edge as it rose into the night until, compressed by distance, only the thorn trees clung to the lowest rim of light. The scent of the acacia blossom and the sorcery of the night had made me almost drunk and I'd half-expected to see rents in the fabric of the moon made by the acacia thorns, for up close the acacias have long thorns, some straight, some recurved like a predator's tooth.

'Paul ...?' said Eva sleepily.

'Yes?'

'How was the moon?'

'Wonderful. Did I wake you?'

'No, I woke myself. What are you thinking?'

'Why?'

'I can feel you thinking something.'

'I'm thinking about the moon. And about something I felt when we were driving up yesterday.'

'What?'

I thought of the feeling of unity, of conjoinment I'd felt, looking at the landscape; the feeling I'd had of holy awe when I saw the moon. But I said: 'It's hard to explain.'

I heard the sheets rustle as she moved. 'Daddy and I often went to watch the full moon when I was little. It was our moon. We never shared it with anyone.'

'Oh?'

'Yes, and no one knew, ever, where we went.'

'Really?

'No, not ever. Now you've seen all this, you do understand about me, don't you?'

'Understand?'

'Yes. About me and the bush.'

'A little,' I said, wondering if she was able to distinguish fantasy from reality, or if she was going to try to force me to see the bush through her eyes, and damn me as disloyal if I disagreed.

'Take Kalilombe for example,' she said. 'He was my sort of mother. He looked after me when I was a baby; he saved me from a puff-adder once, you know.'

'Good Lord, how?'

'Oh, we were walking along one of those narrow game paths, me in front. I wanted to go to a mango tree I knew, to get fruit. And there was this absolutely huge puff adder lying on the path the way they do, to get the heat, and just as I was about to step on it Kalilombe just sort of picked me up with one hand and clouted the snake to death with his stick in the other.'

'Good lord, delivered from serpents.'

'Yes, and I mean, I was brought up here,' she said, warming to her story. 'This was my playground, my garden; it all belonged to me –' Her voice encompassed the whole bush, the whole sky. 'Because it all belonged to Daddy.'

'Oh, yes?' I said. 'Daughter of the son of heaven?'

There was silence. She liked to see herself in a dramatic, mythic way and disliked it when I would not play along. 'You are a shit at times,' she said.

'Why? Because I won't believe your daddy is related to God just a little more intimately than Jesus?'

'You're such a small-minded little shit,' she said bitterly. 'Justin isn't. He understands.'

'Does he? I wonder. Knowing his type, I think he'd humour you just to get into your pants.'

'Fuck off; just fuck off,' she said and I heard the sheets rustle angrily as she turned her back on me.

I closed my eyes and cursed myself. Why couldn't I just play along? Why did I feel that her fantasies threatened the whole universe? That agreeing with her would be a final unredeemable betrayal? No answer came from the night, and thinking these thoughts I went to sleep with the light of the full moon through the open tent flap crawling like a scorpion across my face.

★

Where the waves broke close inshore, the phosphoresence was white in the night. Mandy sighed and stood up and walked to the rail and folded her arms and leant on them, looking out to sea. Her bottom was a twin mound in the tight skirt.

'Look,' she said, pointing out to sea. 'There's a ship.'

I looked out to sea. There was a firefly cocoon of light way out, heading north. I fetched the binoculars and we watched the small freighter dipping its bow into the groundswell, lifting and pitching back down again.

'Let's go inside,' said Mandy. 'It's getting a bit chilly.'

'Oughtn't I to drive you home?'

'Not yet. Mummy's gone to movies, I've got ages still.'

We went inside. She asked for a liqueur and I opened a bottle of Petite Liquorelle and poured a small glass for her. She wandered around the room, touching things, swinging her bottom to tease me, setting her weight into one hip and then the other to show off her legs. She stopped by the elephant tusk and ran her hand down its length.

'Why did you shoot the elephant?'

'We had to.'

'Why?'

'He'd been wounded by poachers.'

'So?'

'It's not easy to explain.'

She walked over to me, hitched up her skirt and straddled me where I sat in my armchair. Her pale thighs were splayed, the tendons drawing taut in her groin.

'Please tell me,' she said softly into my ear. I could smell Ma Griffe again. I tried to ignore her, but it wasn't easy. So close.

'It's not easy,' I said.

She smiled, wriggled a little on my lap and said, 'Tell me, or I'll make you suffer ...'

For a long time I said nothing, listening to the sea, holding her tight against my chest. I remembered how I'd woken the next morning: 'Bwana?'

'Yes?' I answered, still asleep.

'It is morning bwana. I have brought you tea ...'

'Thank you Kalilombe.'

'It is not Kalilombe, bwana, it is Juma. Kalilombe is by the fire.'

'Thank you Juma. What time is it?'

'Four o' clock, bwana.'

'Juma?'

'Yes, bwana?'

'Please don't call me bwana.'

'Yes, bwana.'

Eva slept on. I stood and watched her sleep. Her hair was tumbled around her face, her hands were cupped together beneath her chin like a child's and despite the surge of love I felt watching her, I wondered if anything had happened between her and Justin.

I knew she was always flattered by the attention of young men and this particular young man was dangerously attractive: dark, athletic, tall and amoral. He also made a pretense of being sensitive and sexually adventurous. I felt a momentary foreboding. How often, lapping up her vaginal lubricants, had that savoury brew contained the issue of another man's rod? There was no answer to that question. I watched her sleep. Nothing she did seemed able to quell the love I felt for her. Love makes weaklings of us all. I wanted to wake her to say goodbye but decided that was selfish.

'Don't just sit there looking sad; tell me,' insisted Mandy. So I told her.

I dressed, kissed Eva goodbye as she slept, took the .404 and my small backpack and went out and joined Kalilombe, shivering, at the small, thin-smoking fire of last night that flared mauve-vermilion as he kicked the long mopane logs together to make heat. White ash fell softly. The .416 Rigby leant against a nearby tree.

'Who's Kalilombe?' asked Mandy.

'The tracker.'

'Go on.'

The mug of tea was warm in my hands. I looked at Kalilombe, who sat close to the fire, malarial tremors shaking him. I murmured a good morning but he ignored me. Why was he so silent? I had heard him speak, he had spoken to me. He understood English well enough, but now he would not utter a word. He squatted there baboonlike by the fire, arms resting on his knees, wrists hanging baboonlike down towards the heat, watching the little flames flicker like lovers' tongues about the logs. Perhaps he was mourning his lost wife. I finished my tea in silence and tossed the dregs into the fire.

'Come,' said Kalilombe. He stood and picked up the Rigby. I shouldered Bobs's rifle and followed him. As the light rose I saw his thin shanks moving inside his absurd shorts and the long unmuscled calves at work inside his shiny black skin. I stumbled in the dark.

'Where are we going?'

'To see zebra,' he said in a whisper without turning. 'Then north, Plain of Darkness.'

'What zebra?'

'Lion kill last night,' still without turning.

'Have you got a map?'

'No map of Plain of Darkness,' he said briefly. 'Map here.' He tapped his head.

I was not succeeding very well at the smalltalk so I concentrated instead on not falling over in the dark. This was not easy because the cool night had condensed mist that floated at knee height, hiding the ground and moving heavily like the sea as we waded through it. I wondered about snakes. Were toothy serpents lying in wait? Lion with stump-teeth driven by hunger to eat people like me, leopards?

The pace Kalilombe set was not fast and I was able to keep up easily. I thought I saw him from time to time cast small sideways glances behind; not precisely at me, but past me, to see if I was coping. I found this touching. We were descending now and the light grew even dimmer. I stumbled, almost fell, grabbed for a tree and felt thorns bite deep, swore softly. The ground mist now hovered a foot above my head. The air was cold and damp, as if we had moved beneath the earth into the dwelling place of hobgoblins and elves. The dark was all about us, the way underfoot unsure. I was adrift, rudderless. Somewhere along the road, I thought, I have lost the straight path, I have surrendered hegemony, and something old and harsh has assumed control. Fate? Or the will of the Eumenides keeping the universe in check?

And then I knew: I had somehow called up wild spirits, the Furies had been roused. It may have been the witch at the roadside, but whatever the agent, there were presences everywhere, ghosts of what might have been, of what could be.

I understood then that the savannah, the trees and wooded grasslands of Africa are all peopled by ghosts. For the first time I saw the world with primitive eyes. Those tantalizing heatwaves are souls, not furnace air; the mirages also: not topsy-turvy images upended by heat but spirits shucked from their corporeal husks and freed to dance in the wind, igniting the light with their need to speak. Africa is inhabited by the dead.

There are ghosts of those who ruled before Allah or Jesus, who knew no Christian softness but governed with tact, understanding and a brutality unrivalled even by the Romans in decline. Ghosts of sailors from beyond the sunrise who dared the Sea of Zanj and died, their bones picked clean by ocean currents; explorers who died from tsetse or malaria or snakebite or bloodpoisoning or lion or leopard or buffalo or despair. Elephant hunters who took one shot too many, victims of misfires or shoddy aim or the unseen bull who came from behind. Missionaries who believed their god would protect them, not noting what He'd once done to His own son. Slavers, ambushed by vengeful tribesmen; slaves who died by the side of the endless roads to Mombasa, their hearts broken; imperialists who mistook native politeness for acquiescence and shuffled off their mortal coils pierced through with native iron.

Arabs, Chinese, Dutch, German, Spanish, English, French, Egyptian, Bemba, Kikuyu and Maasai, Shona and Matabele, Zulu and Greek: they all nourished the soil of Africa with their eight pints of blood and a handful of dust. Gone forever, except for their unliberated souls. Perhaps Africa is an ante-room to Hell. Vergil would have felt at home here. And Dante; don't forget Dante.

But as the day grew brighter and our path turned in wide gyres to the floor of the caldera, the early sun burnt off the groundmist and the light crept up between the shuttering trees, and I began to feel more at peace. The ghosts were there, yes; but they were not antagonistic.

'Look,' whispered Kalilombe.

Startled from my dreaming I stopped and looked where he pointed, expecting, befuddled by daydreams, to see a ghost. At first I saw nothing; just the bush, a small clearing, dull and dusty. Then I noticed the vultures perched heavily in the trees, shoulders hunched like sulking cardinals, necks craning downwards; then the ragged carcase of a zebra, legs splayed, teeth bared in a jolly horsey rictus, bowels emptied in a wide dark stain of half-digested grass; then the lions. There were four of them: a big black-maned male, a young female, a juvenile male with a scrubby half-mane and a fully grown lioness, loose shouldered and arrogant.

'Wind good,' whispered Kalilombe, trickling a handful of sand through his fingers. The dust blew towards us. 'We go closer . . . Look.' He slowly lowered the Rigby from its resting place on his shoulder and in a half-crouch began to move closer to the lions. I followed, my heart beating wildly. As we approached I noticed there were hyena too, lying in the shade or silhouetted amongst the scrubthorn, watching the lions with their gargoyle's eyes; and small jackals, heads apologetically lowered, trotting on quick feet to and fro, stopping to look with their foxy tails held low.

We were perhaps thirty yards away from the carcase when the biggest lioness saw us. She was at the rectal end of the zebra, facing us, her muzzle bloody, gnawing with obvious relish at the thick yellow fat around the animal's anus.Her eyes, at first unfocused, fixed us. Her whole facial expression changed. She was suddenly alert and aware. Her ears went up and she became quite still; her shoulders tautened and then, so fast I could almost not follow, she came for us.

The strange slowing of lived time that occurs when we face great danger took over. She was no longer the indolent sexy creature I'd seen in zoos. This was an electrifyingly quick animal, heavy shouldered, big-pawed, bristling with teeth. The other lions looked up, startled. The young female stood but the big male simply stared at us.

The charging lioness was a tawny mass centred about a bone-white snarl of teeth. I heard a deep growl as she charged in a heavy-footed, blindingly fast rush. I shouted. Kalilombe raised his rifle to his shoulder. I did the same, saw the shallow vee of the Express sight settle around the front-sight bead. I slid off the safety.

She was coming straight towards us and I clearly remember the puffs of dust her paws made. Kalilombe fired. The jackals scattered. Shocked vultures took clumsily to the air. The hyenas ducked. The bullet made an explosion of dirt to the left of the lioness and she abruptly swerved, stopped, stumbled and sat clumsily back on her haunches like a big housecat. My mouth was dry, my heartbeat wild. Kalilombe worked the bolt of the rifle. From the corner of my eye I saw the sun catch the ejected cartridge in a bright brassy highlight. The lioness fixed us once with a tense yellow stare and then, with an irritable upward flick of her tail, she turned and sauntered lazily back to the zebra, pausing to nuzzle the big male in greeting.

The other lions watched us for a moment, but one by one grew bored and began to feed again. My heart was beating so hard I felt choked, unable to breathe. I discovered that I was grinning, a broad tooth-bared grin of excitement and fright. I saw Kalilombe glance at me. He motioned me calmly back with the flat of his hand. Walking backwards, eyes fixed on the lions, we slowly retreated. When we were fifty yards from them I let out my breath.

I felt very alive. I could smell the air, detect in it the separate scents of grass and dust and fecal matter and dried blood from the zebra carcase. There was a tinkle in my blood as if I'd drunk off a large glass of cold champagne. Kalilombe smiled at me.

'Thank you for that,' I said.

He shook his head. 'She was going to stop,' he said, as if the syntax were very complex.

'What?'

'She will stop,' he said. 'The bullet was nothing.'

'What?'

'What means a bullet to a lion?' he said and grinned at me, showing very pink gums and an array of snaggle teeth. I stared at him. My knees began to shake.

'My golly!' said Mandy. 'Weren't you frightened?'

'Very,' I said. 'But I only realised how frightened much later.'

'And then what happened? Did you find the elephant?'

'Wait, I'm coming to that part . . .'

Kalilombe said: 'Come,' and walking off at a tangent we skirted the small clearing and the lions and entered the treeline that bordered the far slope of the caldera. For a long time we climbed through high yellow grass with scattered acacia thorns and tall candelabra-shaped cactus. In the grass there was a smell of dust and heat and a scent of wild sage so sharp it burnt in the sinus. The sun was hot and sweat started to bead my face. As we neared the summit I turned and looked back into the pit of the volcano. The lions were still feeding, made small by distance, and the vultures still sulked in the trees. I could not see the jackals or the hyena.

'Look,' said Kalilombe. He was standing on a tall boulder on the top of the rise. I scrambled up beside him and there, stretched as far as I could see, was a wide, empty sea of pale yellow grass. Through my binoculars I could see large herds of wildebeest and zebra. In the distance four giraffe browsed on a stand of thorn trees. A troop of baboons foraged on the edge of the savannah. Cloud shadows chased each other across the plain.

'Plain of Darkness,' he said shortly. 'We sit, look.' He squatted down on the rock and his calloused hands, like the worn paws of an old dog, rooted in the pocket of his olive green tunic and emerged with a small piece of newspaper which read: 'Xmas Beer Shortage: President Appeals For Calm.' He found coarse local tobacco in his shirt pocket and began to roll a cigarette. His eyes did not leave the plain for a second.

I remembered the cigar Bobs had given me and offerred it to Kalilombe but he shook his head, so I bit off the end and lit it myself. It tasted good, the flavour soft and sweet. The fragrant smoke was carried away by the wind. When Kalilombe had tamped down the tobacco to his satisfaction he sealed the cigarette with spittle and set fire to the resultant soggy tube and for the first time I smelt the sour smell of thick wet African shag, coarse and wild, that has ever since turned my heart head over heels with yearning for the bush whenever I have smelt it. We sat together on the summit and smoked in comfortable silence, watching the wind blow soft shadows through the yellow grass.

Finally, Kalilombe pinched off the glowing coal of his fag and stowed the butt away in his top pocket. He stood and shouldered the Rigby. I stretched and picked up the .404. 'Come,' he said, and began the steep descent. I followed, the weight of the rifle heavy on my shoulder.

SEVEN

'The Plain of Darkness,' said Mandy softly. 'It sounds very weird. Was it weird? You know, ghosts and stuff?'

'Yes, weird. And ghosts; but not horror film ghosts. They were just ... there. Presences.'

'I know. I know all about that,' she said. 'Go on ...'

When we reached the Plain of Darkness we walked into the grass at the bottom of the hill, the small volcanic rocks hard and irritating under my boots, the sun high now, heat mounting, sweat running in thin rivulets down my back and into the cleft of my buttocks.

The grass hissed at every step, I remembered, and was high above my head and the wind blew through the seed-heads and dried the sweat on my face and back. Sunlight ran in a bright silken shimmer down each grass stalk and straight into the earth and from the earth back into your body through the soles of your boots. We walked on under a burnished sky that hurt your eyes when you looked at it. Then the going was easier with fewer rocks underfoot as we walked, the sun diagonally to our right, north-east towards the treeline I'd seen from the summit of the ridge.

Dust and seeds and the smell of hot grass and acrid gun oil, occasionally the farmyard smell of buffalo and their dried cow-patty dung in amongst the grass, the tiny date-like droppings of giraffe, kicked-over khaki middens on the edge of dense treed thickets where a rare black rhino had defecated, and old abandoned antbear holes where busily trotting wart-hogs had made their homes.

Sometimes we came to greener trampled-down places amongst the tall grass where bleached bones were scattered, the site of lion kills or wild-dog kills or hyena kills. Picking up a gnawed scapula I saw where the tiny needle teeth of lion cubs had pierced the thin bone. As we walked I saw more and more clusters of white bones, skulls, cracked femurs, ribs. We were in a place of death and I was reminded of the shed where I'd seen all the rhino skulls. Every hundred yards through the grass we came upon a skull, eyesockets vacant, teeth bared in a final grin, crisp sun-dried fragments of skin sticking to the dry bone. Despite the high sun I felt cold. Surrounded by skulls, I felt I was walking amongst the dead. I glanced at my guide. He seemed unmoved; so I followed, taking heart from his indifference.

It took us four hours to cross the Plain of Darkness, I told her, and all the time we walked I thought that we were lost. In the grass there was no way to steer except by the sun and I once again asked Kalilombe if he had a map. I remember his reply very clearly. He stopped walking and turned to me, face blank, and said: 'No map of Plain of Darkness,' and tapped my forehead. 'Your map here,' he said. 'Your map here . . .' and turned and walked on.

'Kalilombe sounds nice. What use was a tracker, though?' asked Mandy.

'My guide.'

'But what was he tracking?'

'Nothing.'

'Carry on . . .' she said and rested her head down on my chest.

All the while we were in the grass there were big birds turning in wide circles overhead. Their dark shadows flashed across the grass ahead of us but when I looked up they were gone in the sun. Once an old lone buffalo bull kneed himself heavily up out of a shallow mud-wallow and galloped away, neck stretched out ahead of him, horns swung low and recurved like a longbow. He stopped and turned a hundred yards away to peer at us, wet nose working to catch our scent. We did not see lion but everywhere there were the chalk white droppings of hyena, matted with half-digested fur. I pointed them out to Kalilombe and he nodded and made a sweeping gesture to his left.

'Fisi there, watching,' he said, and smiled.

But they weren't behind us, they were waiting for us up ahead on the white sandy beach of a shallow river that rolled sluggishly along. The high sun turned the water to hot white steel. There were uprooted trees lying in the water, and cormorants and a lone fish eagle perched there watching for prey. On the far bank a grove of fever trees showed sulphur yellow in the hot light. There were three hyena, staring at us intently as we approached. Cicadas shrilled in the heat.

'Fisi,' said Kalilombe and shook his head. 'Fisi animal for the dead,' he added, a long speech for him. He clearly disliked hyena and I could understand why. I had the strange feeling they were guarding the river because they did not run when we approached but stood and stared at us as if in recognition. The largest took a small step towards us and Kalilombe raised the Rigby smoothly and fired to scare them off. The loud smack-boom of the shot surprised me. He'd shot wide and a splash erupted in the water and the three hyena made off unhurriedly, watching us over their shoulders. The fish eagle took off and called its bleak cry. The hyena stopped fifty yards off in the shade of an ironwood tree and sat down and watched us with interest as we prepared to cross the river.

Kalilombe took off his boots and rolled up his shorts. I did the same.

'Crocs?' I asked.

Kalilombe shook his head. 'Water too little,' he murmured and waded into the shallows. I hoped he was right. The water was bloodwarm and the bottom shelved gradually from sand to mud. Midway the river reached my knees, and then we were climbing the steeper far bank in the shade of a tall silent sycamore fig. We sat in the pleasant shade and dried our feet, and replaced our socks and boots.

'You wait,' said Kalilombe and handed me the Rigby to hold. He walked the short distance to the tall sycamore fig and stared up at the tree. High up, a busy group of green pigeons fed noisily on the ripe fruit. Kalilombe fell to his knees and clapped his hands softly and covered his face and began to speak quietly into his hands, rocking slightly as if in pain and making a thin keening noise that was bereft of all hope. Embarrassed, I turned away and watched the river. On the far bank the hyenas stood, still watching us. A heat shimmer rose from the white sand of the river bank. The murmur of Kalilombe's voice stopped and I turned back and he was standing staring up at the tree again in silence. There were

116

tears on his face which he did not wipe away. The tree stood high and cool and silent. After a moment he turned to me, took the Rigby and said, 'We go.'

I turned and looked back and caught a swift movement out of the corner of my eye, something dark and quick, gone so fast I thought I had seen nothing. For a moment I had the feeling that Bobs was close, that he had followed us and as we walked I frequently turned but I did not see any movement again.

★

The sun was low through the trees by the time we reached camp. At first I could see only a thin column of slaty blue wood-smoke rising straight up through the trees but as we drew nearer I saw the tents and movement, and then the battered khaki Land Rover parked under a tall mopane tree. Kalilombe called out: 'Hodi!' and a happy answering call came: 'Karibu!'

We walked into camp and I was delighted to see my canvas camp chair set beside a small collapsible table. A folding canvas and wood washstand stood by the tent-flap and to one side, neatly positioned on a tarpaulin, was my green canvas camp bath. They'd shot an impala on the way up and the skinner was working on the carcase where it was hung, head down on a slack neck, from the handy branch of an acacia thorn. He'd opened the belly and pulled out the slippery guts in a swollen blue pile, cut through the thorax and pulled out the heart and yellowish lungs and was flecking away the skin now and it swung down heavy and wet from the smooth muscled flesh. Blood thickened in a red pool beneath the carcase.

My feet felt very sore and every muscle ached. I lowered my rifle from my shoulder and rested the butt on my boot while the camp staff clustered around, the skinner included, his hands bloody, knife-blade bloody, all talking at once and pointing to the north, all making big sweeping gestures indicating the size of the elephant's ivory.

'What do they say?' I asked.

'The elephant is there, in the trees, one hour maybe two hours away.'

'When do we go?'

'No time tonight. Sleep first,' Kalilombe said firmly. 'Tomorrow early we go.'

The sun went down dark red as if it had burnt a hole through the sky. Kalilombe's tent and those of the other camp staff had been pitched a discreet distance from mine. They'd built me a tall camp fire and shovelled a bed of hot pink coals to one side to make a cooking fire and the skinner presented me shyly with two impala fillets in a covered dish. I accepted one and donated the other to the staff.

Now I soaped myself in hot water in my canvas camp bath and looked up at the great tropical stars that glowed as softly as fireflies. I could smell the sweet smoke from the thornwood fire, and the rich aroma of grilling impala fillet. The sky in the west was the colour of a bruised over-ripe peach. I wondered what Eva was doing and felt an acute and hopeless longing for her.

After supper and a whisky I rummaged in my small pack and found my worn old briar pipe and a dark Latakia tobacco and smoked a pipefull by the fire, watching the stars arc slowly across the sky. I sensed Kalilombe before I saw his dark figure just outside the circle of the firelight.

'Kalilombe?'

He stepped into the light. His eyes were fixed on mine.

'What can I do for you?'

He watched me in silence for a time, then said, 'Tomorrow we will walk early. Very early.'

'Yes?'

He shifted uneasily. 'It is not easy to hunt the elephant ...'

'No. So?'

'We must be the elephant.'

'Oh yes? And how do we do that?'

He shook his head. 'I cannot tell you ... but I give you this ...' He handed me a small carefully bound sachet of skin the size of a teabag.

'What's this, Kalilombe?' I said, turning it over in my hands.

'Samba. It is mankhwala.'

'Mankhwala? Samba? What's samba,' I asked, a little irritably.

'Samba is the one that eats ants. He digs deep down, where it is dark. Medicine for dreams,' he said abruptly. Then he turned and walked away.

I sat and pondered this, turning the little sachet of skin between my fingers. I was not at all certain what to make of it. Later when Orion was high I climbed into my sleeping bag and left the tent flap open so I could see the moon. I put the little amulet of anteater skin on the floor beside the rifle. Sleep came quickly.

I woke once in the night when a quick shower of rain came, pattering on the tent fly and hissing on the coals of the fire. Far away I heard hyena whooping and felt for the .404 by my side and turned over and went to sleep again.

In sleep a dream came to me. Lying snug and secure in my tent the soft clatter of rain on the canvas transformed me suddenly into the elephant we had come to kill. As the elephant I heard the same rain splatter on mopane leaves, felt the same rain cold on my back and spine, clotting the dust into mud that ran in thin rivulets down my flanks. I smelt the hot slaked dust in my trunk, smelt my own spilt blood, felt the rain drip wet down my belly, knew the damp squelch of mopane leaves under my feet. And I knew the loneliness and pain too; the burning heat in my lung, the slow choke as blood seeped from torn arteries and I began to drown, the working of a broken rib in my flesh, the grate of jagged bone on broken bone-end where the bullet had smashed through my shoulder. The pain and anger grew in me and I turned and charged the first person I saw. As I bore down on her, intent to kill, I saw it was Eva. Beside her, her father raised his rifle and I heard the boom of the shot and felt the sudden impact of the bullet in my forehead. Blood filled my vision and I saw then that the man holding the rifle had become the dark young hunter, Justin. I saw his teeth bared white in a big grin and then I was dead.

'What an awful dream,' said Mandy. 'Was it the mankwhat-ever?'

'Who knows. I gave it back to Kalilombe. He didn't say a word.'

'And who's Justin?'

'A young hunter. Rather good looking.'

119

'Did Eva like him?'

'In a manner of speaking,' I said, but she missed the irony.

'And then? What did you do next? Did you find the elephant? '

Kalilombe woke me at four and I dressed quickly and washed the sleep from my eyes with icy water from the canvas basin outside the tent before joining him at the small fire. The rain had not doused the strong-burning thornwood in the night and he'd knocked coals from the logs and brewed strong tea thick with condensed milk which we sipped from enamel mugs. Well before dawn we were on our way, the .404 now a familiar weight on my shoulder, sore muscles warming as we walked.

We didn't find the elephant that day, nor the next, nor the day after that. We found spoor, some quite fresh, most a day or two old. When we found spoor early, we walked on it for hour after hour in the furnace heat at a pace I found hard at the beginning to maintain. But after four days my feet were hardened and I'd leaned down a little and I was able to keep up with Kalilombe; but still we didn't find the elephant. Each dusk we'd arrive back in camp to be greeted by eager queries from the camp staff, only to disappoint them. After seven days of fruitless hunting we needed camp meat and Kalilombe took me out with the safari's small .275 Rigby to shoot an impala.

We found a herd of females led by a dominant male who had lovely horns, widening at the top, his coat smooth, his haunches plump. They were browsing in a small clearing beneath a stand of lofty ebony trees whose dark trunks gave the clearing a sombre air, like the inside of the cathedral. Although the wind was good, the impala sighted us – aided by a querulous grey loerie shouting 'G'way! G'way!' – and trotted off warily but unperturbed for fifty yards. The male herded his harem ahead of him, then paused on a grassy tumulus and looked back at us over his shoulder.

'Now,' whispered Kalilombe.

I knelt and raised the little Rigby and as the cross-hairs settled just behind his shoulder, I squeezed the trigger. The Rigby gave a sharp small-calibre crack and the impala went down, legs kicking. The females scattered in panic; within days they'd accept a new master.

Kalilombe ran ahead of me, fast as a dog, and knelt beside the impala. He nodded in satisfaction. 'Dead,' he muttered, and cut the throat with his folding knife. Hot blood ran out of the severed arteries and into the soil. I had never killed any living thing before. I felt hollowed out inside. I stroked the impala's flanks. He was warm still, and firm, his muscles almost alive under my touch and I felt a deep sadness, tempered with relief that I'd killed him cleanly and well. Kalilombe handed me his knife.

'Gut and skin,' he said abruptly. I knelt and made the first incision around the neck, sensing Kalilombe's eyes critically watching every move I made with the knife. My hands were soon covered with blood.

Perhaps this was some sort of test. The next day Kalilombe struck camp and sent the rest of the safari back to Coletrane's headquarters. 'We must hunt alone. We cannot find the elephant if we come home every night like old women,' he said. 'We must walk, sleep, walk early, sleep, walk again, then we find him.'

And that is what we did. Taking only a small tent fly and a groundsheet the two of us hunted after the old bull, staying on his trail as he wound his slow way up towards the eastern escarpment, never straying far from water, never resting long enough for us to catch up with him. And all the time we walked, Kalilombe talked – softly, carefully – about the bush around us. I learnt to identify where baboons had found grubs beneath the prised-up bark of dead trees; to recognise the anthracite droppings of pangolins, full of the iridescent black carapaces of ten thousand ants; where to find water in the hollow trunk of a baobab; and how to make coffee from the small berries of the buffalo-thorn tree.

At night we pitched camp, lit a small fire and ate mposho meal and impala meat that Kalilombe had smoked over a greenwood fire. Even if we hadn't fired a shot, he insisted we clean the rifles every night, using the small pull-through he kept in an old cigarette tin. At first I regarded this as a silly chore, but then I realised the rifles were our survival tools; they deserved every care we could give them. Sometimes I'd drink a small whisky, sometimes smoke a pipe, and Kalilombe would sometimes construct one of his wild-smelling cigarettes; and then we'd fall asleep quickly, side by side under the light tent fly, listening to the bush sounds all around, too exhausted to wonder if a hyena would come in the night and bite off our faces. Each morning we drank hot sweet tea and struck camp and were back on the trail well before dawn, the bush eerie in the chill grey light. By now we had grown to know each other. We moved as one; I found that I anticipated Kalilombe's thoughts, and he mine. We spoke little.

Just before sunup on the twelfth day we found the first fresh sign of elephant we'd seen for days: broken acacia branches and warm dung that steamed in the pre-dawn coolness. Kalilombe stooped and inserted a finger into the largest, nodded and went forward more slowly. I could hear the crack of breaking branches. They were up ahead to our left, upwind, a group of cows and calves browsing on tall winterthorns and soft short grass. As I watched, the largest cow curled her trunk round and round a tuft of grass in a corkscrew action, uprooted it, and with a delicate sideways swing of her forefoot neatly sheared off the roots and soil against her tusk.

Kalilombe moved around the feeding herd well to the right, not wanting to spook them in case the wounded bull was nearby. But he needn't have bothered because it was almost midday before we picked up his spoor, wide deep depressions in the sand that were twice as large as any footprints I'd seen before.

'When?' I asked.

He shrugged and shook his head slightly. 'Four, maybe five o'clock. While we drink tea.'

'How far ahead?'

'Not so far. He is sick with pain. See, that foot is sore,' he said, pointing to the spoor. There was a clear drag mark from the right front leg. I nodded, remembering my dream.

'See, poachers shoot him here,' he said, holding his arm above the elbow. 'It is hot now, he will stand under trees and sleep, later go to water. We find him soon ...'

'Do we shoot him?'

He frowned. 'We will see. If he is in great pain, yes, we must shoot him, and he will be happy to die. But if he is not so sick, we leave him, maybe dart him later, bring vet.'

'But if we don't shoot him, he may kill more people.'

He shrugged. 'Better save one elephant than ten people.'

He pulled back the bolt of the Rigby, chambered a round and put on the safety. I did the same. He watched me without expression. 'We go,' he said, and walked quietly on ahead.

We found him standing under a tall umbrellathorn tree one hour later. He was huge, twelve feet at the shoulder, big tattered ears moving stiffly in the heat like salt-caked sails. He was clearly very old. His temples were sunken deep and his backbone was a high bony ridge but his tusks were magnificent, two long, pale sap-stained arcs. There was a sovereign-sized bullet hole in his left ear, long healed, and a mud-caked mess of dried blood ran down his chest from a raw dark-red bullet hole. The fierce sun had cauterised the flesh black around the entry and white bone showed deep in the wound. There was more dried blood below his right shoulder, where Kalilombe had said it would be, and he held his right forefoot high, resting it on the toe. Through the binoculars I saw his eyes half closed with pain and I could hear the high relentless whine of big blue flies worrying the dried blood. His tail moved rhythmically.

Kalilombe shook his head, a look of profound sorrow on his face, but said nothing. He moved the big Mauser flag-type safety of the Rigby to the centre and softly withdrew the bolt, checked that the chambered cartridge was a solid and closed the bolt again. He moistened a finger and held it high. The wind was blowing fitfully towards us. We were sixty yards away. In a half-crouch Kalilombe began to move quietly towards the elephant who had turned slightly away from us. I followed, heart beating wildly. We had covered forty yards and Kalilombe was edging to his left to open the angle for a side brain shot when the fickle midday air eddied in a tight corkscrew and blew our scent to the elephant.

He turned slowly, favouring the right leg, raised his trunk and tested the air and in dead silence tucked down his head and charged us. There was no wild trumpeting, no hesitation. He came in quietness. I saw Kalilombe throw up his rifle, heard the crack-boom as he fired, saw the heavy bullet whack a handfull of dust from the bull's head, high up on his forehead. The massive skull was pulled up from the impact of the heavy bullet but it didn't halt his charge.

Possessed, I sensed the lessons learnt so long ago in my grandfather's study take over. I raised the .404, feeling terror and panic shake me, saw the bead settle into the vee of the rearsight and pulled the trigger. The rifle erupted and I saw a bright explosion of blood about a pale-edged hole appear just too high for a brain shot and then the elephant was on me. I felt a blow of immense power strike my shoulder. The rifle spun away, and I felt myself fly through the air. The whole world was red with blood and I landed in a tangled heap at the bottom of a thorn tree, breath knocked from my lungs. I remember the bull rearing above me, huge and dark, with his ears spread wide like death with open wings; then I fainted.

The elephant's loud enraged squeals penetrated my brain and I came to and found myself being hurled left and right. I opened my eyes and through a veil of blood saw the bull's massive head poised over me. I can clearly remember the incredibly long eyelashes. Bright arterial blood spurted in finger-thick arcs from the wounds in his forehead. His tusks were planted on either side of my body and he was trying to crush me and tusk me but the sand was soft and his tusks too long. I felt ribs crack and then a tusk ripped between bicep and bone. From far off I heard myself scream and a desperate rage filled me and I kicked out hard with both legs and the bull stepped back, trumpeting in anger. Blood sprayed in thick clotted gouts from his trunk and covered my face and I smelt a stench of rotting flesh so strong I vomited and then lay still, exhausted, all fight gone.

Suddenly the squealing stopped and I heard a loud crack, like a femur snapping; and with growing awe and fear I saw that the elephant had broken a large branch from a thorn tree. Swaying, the bull stepped towards me and laid the branch gently on my body. I could not scream, could not even whimper; I simply lay there, certain in the knowledge that the bull elephant knew I was going to die. Slowly, with great care, the bull broke off branch after branch and laid them carefully on my body until they were a crushing weight on my chest and I could no longer breathe.

With a final soft trumpet that sprayed blood in tangled clots on the branches, the elephant turned away and left me for dead. As I felt consciousness fade I heard a gunshot and a final distant trumpet. Then everything turned grey and I could see only a long dark passage lined with bare trees. On each tree sat a hunch-shouldered vulture. Then all visions left me and I was not there any more.

EIGHT

'Golly,' said Mandy. 'What happened then?' She hitched her skirt a fraction higher, stared into my eyes. 'What happened to the elephant?'

'Kalilombe shot him.'

'Golly! That's so sad. And you?'

'I was quite sick for a while. I'd lost a bit of blood, and the elephant broke some of my ribs, and to top it all I went down with fever; but Kalilombe built a little hut right there and looked after me.'

'He sounds very nice.'

'He is. Was.'

'Why was?'

'He died.'

'Died? Why? What from?'

'He just died.'

'But why?'

'I'm not sure. I think he died because he wanted to. His wife was killed by a crocodile one day while fetching water and he couldn't accept it. He really loved her. He couldn't talk about it, he didn't have the words. He sort of died because he couldn't talk. He was the saddest person I've ever met. And he taught me so much.'

'Don't you miss him?'

'Of course. Not just because he saved my life; he taught me how to live, I think.'

'That's how you got your tusk?'

'Kalilombe arranged it with the game department. He gave me one and kept the other himself.'

'What'd he do with his tusk?'

'He sold it to an ivory dealer in Juba and gave the money to the anti-poaching unit.'

'Wasn't Eva worried when you were away for so long? Your wife?'

'Not really. Her father persuaded her that we were gone so long simply because we hadn't found the elephant yet. And anyway, there was that young hunter in camp to keep her company.' I like to think I said this without bitterness.

'Who? What hunter?'

'I told you. Justin. Very handsome boy. He looked very like her Daddy when young.'

'You mean she slept with him?' asked Mandy in surprise. When I didn't answer she leant close and stared into my eyes. I stared back at her but the memory still was as fresh as the day Kalilombe and I arrived back in camp with the ivory and Eva came running up, her hair so pale, and I saw in her eyes what she'd done; but worse, that she wanted me to know.

Mandy punched my arm. 'How did you find out?'

I shrugged. 'I think I knew all along; but there was a pair of his underpants under Eva's bed in our tent. And there was a silly letter he'd written that I found. Very descriptive. And all the boys knew. I could tell from the way they looked at me.'

'Boys? What boys?'

'Camp servants.'

'Not real boys.'

'No. It's a silly name.'

'Did she often . . . I mean, was that the first time, or did she always . . .'

'I don't know. She probably did. Who knows? She just couldn't help herself that time. And anyway, it's not all that important, is it?'

'Were you sad?'

Was I sad? The cuckolded husband: no tragedy there, too commonplace. And lost love? Where is the uniqueness in that? Perhaps the sadness lay in the banality of events. I'd vainly tried to believe that we were somehow better, that our love was different. I'd betrayed Eva by being inadequate, not knowing her stresses, caring too little.

Now I'd been both betrayer and betrayed, had felt the scourge, sad cuckold, complaisant lover, deceiver in turn deceived, all too human. At the time, tears of self-pity had taken me. Everyone knows the symptoms: throat choked tight, sobs queuing to be released, the pain impervious to logic, unquelled because unquellable, the anger.

But there was a nascent giggle too. Pomposity pricked always brings a titter. Comedy stalks the tragic actor playing Lear playing at king; guffaws skulk in the stalls when Hamlet talks to a skull, when Othello goes doolally, when Cleopatra asps herself to death. We all like to see the inflated brought low, the common man inhabits us all. That'll teach him, giving himself airs, should've known his place, got what was coming too him, didn't he, see? Take that! The cuckolded husband! No tragedy there.

'Yes,' I said. 'I was sad then, but I'm not any more.'

'Aren't you?' she murmured dubiously, staring at me. 'I think you are.' I hugged her gently, and felt her great generosity of spirit in the way her body relaxed against mine, the way it flowed into mine. I had a strange feeling then that our bodies had become unbounded; as if the limits of limb and torso were corporeal only and that our true bodies extended further, as if there was a tenuous mist of being that commingled like the haze of stars around a distant galaxy when you view it through a telescope. It was a very erotic sensation and I tried to ignore the sexuality of our position and the deep arterial pulse I could feel. I think she had forgotten for a time as well; but now, simultaneous with my own awareness of her splayed legs and her little mound pressed against me, I sensed that she suddenly felt herself ready for release. I heard it in her breathing, felt it in the way she held me.

'Paul . . .' she began softly. 'Wait . . .' She pulled away from me, looked at me with a small smile and said, 'Please hold me . . .' Then she pulled her skirt a little higher and slipped her fingers into the top of her panties.

'No. Mandy!' I said but she ignored me, lying tight against me, left arm locked around my neck. I felt her little fingers working at her groin and she made soft little whimpers of pleasure. Her body was hot, eyes shut tight, her legs quivered. Then with a moan she went slack in my arms and I held her close and tight, feeling my own unreleased pleasure ebb away; but the ache remained.

128

I drove her home in my old Land Rover, which she enjoyed, declaring it much better than Mummy's Jaguar. She chattered happily all the way, thanking me for supper, for oysters, for the wine, for telling her my story about the elephant, for holding her. Her directions were precise and she insisted on showing me where to park in a dark place outside her mother's large double-storey house so she could kiss me goodbye, which she did with an energy and expertise that amazed me. I watched her run up her driveway and turn to wave goodbye in the pool of light from her opened front door. Then the door closed and she was gone. Why did I feel violated?

Back at the beachhouse I finished the bottle of Petite Liquorelle and sat on the porch in the dark and smoked a pipe of rich Macedonian tobacco. Thoughts of onanism: (her long pale legs, the soft swell on the inside of her upper thigh, that taut tendon in her groin, the soft mound of her pubis, her mouth and honey tongue, the smell of her!) I watched the white line of the breakers push in to the beach, pause and retreat.

The Turkish tobacco was sweetly rancid in the night and reminded me of Kalilombe: hunting the elephant, we'd spent many a tired dusk smoking comfortably while night closed on Africa as swiftly as an eyelid. Kalilombe told me later that he was certain the elephant had killed me. He said the mound of branches that covered me was a mass of clotted blood. He scrabbled the branches away and found me pressed into the sand by the elephant, covered in blood and mucous like a stillborn foetus.

He told me the fever was bad; I was incoherent for seven days. But on the seventh, he said, 'the devils left us.' I remember only one thing about that time. I dreamt one night that I was dying. I could feel death as a foreign breath inside me. I could smell it: putrescent, thick with maggots. As the vile breath filled my lungs I saw that there were waterbuck patiently waiting to fetch me away from the hut. They were standing in a small group under a thorntree in the shade, watching me, waiting for me to die so that they could take me with them. Then the dream left me and I woke, feeling grimy and spindle-shanked, thin and burnt down by fever. I found I was lying on a bed of soft cut grass but had no recollection of how I'd got there. The Tuareg cross lay beside me on the earth floor. I put it on. I examined the long thin scar on my arm. It was pink and tender but had healed well. There was no inflammation.

In the shadows I saw the long pale curves of a pair of hundred pound tusks, their bases stuffed with dry grass and bound with cloth and bark string. Although I was weak, my head was quite clear and I stood shakily and opened the door of the hut and looked out, not knowing quite where I was. It was just before dawn and there was a small campfire burning, but Kalilombe was nowhere to be seen. The air was cool after night rain, the thornwood smoke sweet on the breeze. Like a hollowed-out ghost of an elephant, the skull of the big bull we'd shot stood quiet and white near the hut. Of the rest of the skeleton there was no sign. I found the entry holes of Kalilombe's bullets in the skull, and my own, traced their paths and found the cratered exits they'd made.

All about in the soft sand I saw spoor of hyena and lion, drawn by the meat Kalilombe had set out on rough drying racks. There was a mist like the exhalations of a herd of elephants, pale grey and still, lying in quiet clots and eddies in the valley below the hut. And there across the valley, standing shaggy-necked, calm and watchful, was a small group of waterbuck. They were watching me quietly, veiled by mist, their black noses testing the air. The dawn wind moved their thick fur. I watched them watching me. Then the wind changed and the mist moved and they were hidden from view. I still wonder what they were doing there.

I knocked out my pipe, locked up the house, checked to see if Ludwig was sleeping easily, and went to bed.

I was woken by a sound of lamentation, a savage high-pitched keening. For a second, still asleep, I thought it was Kalilombe, the noise was identical to that he'd made kneeling by the giant fig on the banks of the sluggish river, but it was Ludwig. I ran through to the pantry and found him gripped by a fit, his spine bent backwards like a bow, hair erect, teeth gritted in pain, eyes rolled back. I knelt beside him and held him close. Great tremors spread through his body.

I called his name and the howling pitched higher. I began to panic, not knowing what to do: the helplessness. I held him tighter and closer and slowly the shaking calmed. He was hot with fever. I held him until even the tiny shivers had ceased, felt for his pulse and found its weak but regular beat in his armpit. He'd fallen into an exhausted sleep. I brought my duvet and pillows and settled down beside him on the floor and fell asleep with his calm breathing in my ears.

I woke next morning with Ludwig licking my face. He was grinning as only a Labrador can and seemed untouched by his fit. I patted him and told him he was a good dog. He was very weak but revived after a bowl of warm milk and his tablets. I made him comfortable in his basket and went through to the sitting room and opened the blinds and looked out.

The sea was flat calm, the beach deserted. The sky was still pale, the powdery bluegrey of the inside of a mussel shell. I walked out onto the porch. The air was cold so I went inside, found my old sweater, made tea, and took the tray onto the porch and settled into one of the camp chairs to watch the light change and think about the coming day.

I planned to make bouillabaisse for my old friend Charles who was coming to lunch. I'd not seen him for eighteen years and when he'd phoned several weeks ago I was delighted.

'I simply looked up your number in the phone book,' he'd said in answer to my question. 'On an impulse. I can't imagine why I didn't do it before. Silly. I'd been listening to that Haydn cello concerto. Do you remember? The C Major? They found the manuscript in Prague or somewhere in your first year, and I bought that Jacqueline du Pre? Do you remember?'

'Of course! But how are you?'

'Not now. Ask me to lunch and I'll tell you.'

I gave him directions and asked him to bring a friend, wondering what the friend would be like. I felt a little apprehensive. The years between eighteen and thirty six bring decay and I was not certain what Charles would make of the sour bachelor I'd become.

I went through to the kitchen and began to chop carrots and onions and fennel and leeks for the stock, wondering what the day would bring, wondering if Mandy would come.

CODA

In my end is my beginning.

Mary Queen of Scots.

ONE

She came at ten. She was wearing a little white skirt and a pale blue blouse and a dark blue jersey knotted over her shoulders. 'I missed you,' she said, hugging me tightly. 'I thought about you the whole night.'

'Didn't you sleep?'

'Of course. I thought about you in my sleep! How's Ludwig?'

I told her about his fit and she listened closely and decided to phone the vet, who told her that there was no organic reason for Ludwig's convulsions, but that he was an old dog and one should expect odd things like that. This answer satisfied her – if not me – and she sat beside Ludwig, whispering into his ear while he lay in a coma of pleasure, grinning stupidly at her.

'What are you making?' she asked.

'A sort of fish soup. An old friend of mine's coming to lunch. You can stay, if you like.'

'That sounds wonderful. But I can't.' She pulled a face. 'I've got to visit my father, it's his turn today. Can I help you cook? I love cooking.'

'Of course.' I felt disappointed. I'd grown accustomed to her presence and after the strange sensation of the previous night when I'd felt my body dissolve into hers I wanted her close to me all the time. But that was hardly realistic.

She set about cutting monkfish fillets into pieces for the stock. I added kingklip, prawns, a crayfish and two whole silver fish to the stock pot as well as saffron and garlic and a cup of thick green olive oil. Mandy followed my recipe for rouille, energetically pounding chillies with my pestle and mortar. When the stock was simmering I opened an icy bottle of Graves and we went out onto the porch in the thin sun and drank the wine and watched the gulls.

'I've got a surprise for you,' she said presently.

'What?' I asked, not without suspicion.

She reached into the pocket of her blouse and handed me an envelope. I opened it. Inside were six polaroid photographs.

'Who took these?' I asked.

'I did. I propped the camera on the dressing table. It's got one of those timer things. Do you like them? They're for you to keep.'

She'd got the light right by accident rather than design. She was standing in a white-painted bedroom and the white curtains had filtered the sunlight so her body seemed incandescent. She was quite naked, standing looking straight into the camera with her hair backlit into a burning halo. The light made her body seem fuller, rounder. It had filled out her thighs, plumped up her breasts and rounded her buttocks. Her body looked creamy and succulent, her skin syrupy. She had been very thorough.

'Do you like them?' she insisted.

'Yes, of course I do,' I said. 'But I can't possibly keep them.'

'Why ever not? I did them for you.'

'Yes, but I can't.'

'Why not? Give me one good reason why not.'

'They make me uncomfortable.'

'Why? You've seen naked girls before. You've just about seen me naked. You're a photographer, after all.'

'I know.'

'But?'

'But I can't.' I looked at the pictures again. She was very beautiful. She had one of those bodies that look very explicit when naked, defined by function. She looked as if she'd been designed for sexual gratification. It was odd to see that knowledge in such a young body. I'd grown accustomed to seeing models of twenty with bodies like that, full of a fleshly wisdom at odds with their years but acquired by their constant preoccupation with self and physical beauty, refined by constant grooming and the insistent press of desiring male eyes. But this seemed almost an ineradicable genetic memory, a primal sexuality welded into her blood generations before, a promise of ecstasy not within the compass of other women.

136

'Please keep them,' she begged. 'Please. I made them for you.'

'No, Mandy. I'm very flattered, and I'm very grateful to you for showing me. You're very beautiful, very sexy. Your body's lovely.'

'Do you like my nipples? Don't you think they're too big?'

'Not at all.'

'But they cover half my boobs. I think they're too big.'

I shook my head, pressed the polaroids into her hands. 'Trust me,' I said. 'They're not too big, they're perfect.'

'Do you want to see them, to check?' she said, teasing now, pretending to unbutton her blouse.

'No!' I said, backing away, which made her giggle. 'Mandy, listen to me. You can't live your life simply by doing things you know men will like.'

'I don't.'

'Yes, you do. Listen to me: you must do the things you want, not what men want you to do. All this dressing up –'

'But you said you liked it!'

'I do: that's not the point. You can't define yourself by what I like. That's not good enough, you'll make yourself very unhappy, and you'll never know who you are.'

'But you don't understand. I dress for you because I like it for myself; I like to tease you, I feel sexy. And I like to make you think of me as if I'm your wife when I dress up for you the way she did.'

I stared at her and said nothing.

She took my hand in both of hers, turned it palm upwards and stared at it.

'It says here you've got to make love to me,' she said gravely.

'Oh yes?'

'Yes, and look here,' she said, holding up her right palm for me to see. 'Here, on my life line? It says you must make love to me; and here on my fate line it says that if you don't make love to me, I'll be a lost soul forever, condemned to wander the world never finding my own true love.'

'Oh, really.'

'Yes. Don't you believe that?'

'No, Mandy.'

'You see? You don't know anything. We're married. We were married by the sea when we dived on that wreck together. And the dolphins; didn't you see them? Didn't you feel it? I felt it so clearly.'

'Nonsense,' I said firmly. She smiled at me. 'I wish it was nonsense,' she said. 'But I think it's true. I've decided to make love to someone soon, and I'd've liked it to be you. So would the dolphins. But you're stupid, you think it's wrong.'

'It's late,' I said. 'And I haven't collected the mussels for my soup yet.'

She stared at me wryly for a moment and said, 'Come on, then. I'll help you.'

★

'If you're very nice to me, I'll take you to my own private mussel bed,' she said as we walked along the beach.

'That's very kind.'

'I've never taken anyone there before, not even Kate.'

'Who's Kate?'

'My very best friend. She sleeps next to me in the dorm,' she said. 'She's got a crush on me, but I don't mind. It worries Miss Vapour though.'

'Vapour? Who's Miss Vapour'?

'Her name's Faber, actually. She's our housemistress. But I call her Miss Vapour because she's always upset about something. I think she's a virgin. Or a lesbian. Or both. She's worried about Kate and me because she thinks we're lesbians, and that's silly. All we do is make each other come sometimes.' I decided to ignore that.

She led me to her own private secret mussel bed (which happened to be my secret mussel bed too), and we began to collect mussels. We chose carefully, taking the ripe mussels that are elegantly shelled and taste of kelp and the waves. But Mandy was not satisfied. The best mussels of all, she said, were to be found in a pool that was hidden behind an outcrop of boulders: it was very deep and cold and could only be reached when the tide was just right. I had not been there. The gulls wheeled overhead on taut wings, screaming at us as we clambered over the huge tumbled rocks. She led me through a maze of rocks that guarded the entry to her secret bed until we reached a sheltered overhang. She insisted we sit for a while.

'I have to be sure the sea's not too high,' she explained gravely.

138

We sat. The wind had come up and the air had a chill seaborn edge. Mandy huddled close to me and took my hand in hers. The wind blew her hair across my face with the touch of a spirit's fingers. She watched the sea for long minutes then pronounced it safe, 'but not for long.'

'Come on,' she said, pulling me to my feet. 'We must hurry or the sea'll be breaking over the rocks and we won't be able to get any mussels at all!'

It happened while I was stretching my arm down into the clear icy water to pick a mussel. There was a growing rumble and I looked up in fright. One of those massive waves that seem to heave up out of nowhere into sudden huge breakers was bearing down on us. Mandy was on the far side of the pool, close to the sea's edge, her back to the waves. The high tumbling snout of the breaker reared up behind her. I shouted 'Mandy!' She looked up at me, grinned, held up a mussel. Then the wave burst on top of her and she disappeared in an explosion of foam and water.

I dived into the pool against the wave, ducked under and swam towards her. My hands touched her wriggling body and I grabbed a handful of her jersey and kicked for the surface. The water was icy. We burst through the surface, panting. Mandy was retching up sea water, choking and coughing. Her long hair was plastered all over her face. I brushed it away, holding her up, treading water. Through her jersey I could feel her heart patter against my hand like rain; and enveloping the heartbeat was a soft small breast. I removed my hand, pulled her close and held her until her spasm had passed.

'Mandy! Are you hurt?'

She grinned at me, shook her head, held up her mussel.

'Come on.' I said. 'Let's go.' We swam to the side of the now placid pool, collected our mussels and ran back to my house. It was freezing in the sharp wind. She was shivering and I was sure she'd catch cold. As I fumbled my key into the front door with numb fingers I said, 'I hope you don't get pneumonia.'

She shook her head. 'I never even catch cold. Can I have a hot bath? And a jersey of yours? Or a shirt?'

'Of course.' I gave her a big towel. 'Get those wet things off. Use the spare bedroom, I'll run you a bath.'

I ran a hot bath, added Badedas and called her when it was ready. She appeared wrapped in her towel and kissed me quickly on the cheek. 'Thank you for being so kind,' she said.

'Nonsense. Go and bath.'

I found a soft old lambswool jersey and hung it on the bathroom doorknob. She'd half-closed the bathroom door. 'Your jersey's on the doorknob,' I called.

'Thanks!'

I listened to her happy splashing and found her pile of wet clothes in the spare bedroom and rinsed them and put them in the tumble dryer. Her panties were white with little pink hearts. No bra today.

I showered in the glass cabinet next door to the bathroom. I could hear her off-key singing. I realized while in the shower that it was terribly late. Charles was due for drinks at twelve-thirty and it was already quarter to. Half-dry, with a towel knotted around my waist, I went quickly to the kitchen and started to scrub the mussels free of weeds and beard. The bubbling stock smelt rich.

'Where are you?' I heard her call.

'In the kitchen.'

'My hair's still sopping,' she said as she walked in, a towel wrapped turbanlike around her head. My jersey fitted her like a mini dress. She stopped and stared at me. I became uncomfortably conscious of my towel.

'You look just like my Poseidon statue with that beard,' she said in quiet wonder. Then she ran at me full tilt, arms outstretched and small breasts bobbing beneath the jersey and threw her arms around me.

'Thank you for saving me in the pool,' she said softly. I hugged her chastely. 'That's fine, Mandy.'

'Please can I have a kiss?'

'A kiss?' I said nervously.

'Yes. I want to give you a thank you kiss.'

'Fine.'

I bent and tried to kiss her quickly but she lifted herself right off the floor by her arms that she locked round my neck and forced her mouth clumsily but effectively against mine. Her tongue flickered between my lips.

'Stop it, Mandy!' I said.

'Sorry.' But she grinned up at me unrepentant. I pushed her firmly away and returned to the mussels.

And then all her casual bending over without her pants on to reveal the soft full swell of her bottom and ineffectual tugging at the hem of the jersey, and crossing of almost childlike legs to give the briefest flash of pubic shadow was seduction, and she gloried in it. I felt the tension of engorgement, which is difficult to conceal while wearing a towel, and knew that she, with her frightening female knowledge, was delighted with the effect she'd had on me. But she was fourteen. Not sixteen, not fifteen even. Fourteen. Thirteen and three-quarters. It was impossible. I don't know what she expected. I could see the signs of teenage arousal in her: bright eyes, slack mouth, the soft, uneven breathing. It would've been comic if it hadn't been so frightening.

I finished cleaning the mussels, transferred them fussily to a pot, added white wine, rosemary and garlic and set them to one side. I decided to be frank.

'Mandy?' I said.

'Yes?' She turned quickly, managing to bump my hip with hers. When had she moved so close?

'Mandy, I think you should get dressed now,' I said. 'Your clothes are in the tumble dryer.' I turned her around by her shoulders and marched her to the door. She went obediently, which should have alerted me. I found I was sweating slightly. I decided it would be wise to put on a tape, something gentle, that Beethoven Quintet, opus twenty something. I walked through to the sitting room and found Mandy standing there, her arms full of her clothes which she dropped as I entered the room. She was wearing nothing but a pair of tiny black silk panties. She bent, pulled down the panties and kicked them away so that I could see the whole beautiful length of her, quite naked, from the top of her tousled head to the tips of her clumsily painted toenails. I stared at her. Her breasts were fuller than I'd thought, her nipples wide and pink, veined like a stone, her thighs inviting touch, pliant, limber, the curves of waist and hip more generous than a child's, the weight of her pudendum pale through the blond pubic hair.

'Do you like me?' she said in a quiet voice.

'Yes,' I said, hearing my own voice from far away.

'Good,' she said, and walked towards me. I did not move.

TWO

At that moment the doorbell rang. My friend Charles, uncharacteristically early. The noise sobered me.

'Go and dress,' I whispered. 'Quickly!' She laughed at me, gathered up her clothes and ran through to my bedroom, buttocks dancing, tiny furred purse tight between her thighs. I tightened my towel around my waist and opened the front door. The likeness was remarkable. She wore a crisp white summer frock.

'Hello,' she said. 'I'm Barbara Thetiss. I'm sorry to bother you, but I think you know my daughter Mandy?' I saw her stare at my towel.

'Mandy? Yes, of course.'

'May I talk to her for a moment?'

I stared at her. I could think of nothing to say.

'She is here?' she asked, puzzled.

'Here?' I stared at her. 'Here?'

'Yes, here. She said she was coming to visit you. You have a sick dog. Ludwig. I phoned you one morning. Do you remember?'

'Sick dog. Ludwig. Yes, yes. Please come in,' I said, standing to one side.

'Thank you. I'm sorry to just arrive on your doorstep like this,' she said, chatting politely, 'but I did try to phone earlier and there was no reply.'

'Ah,' I said brightly. 'We were collecting mussels.'

She nodded. 'You see, Mandy's father's expecting her for lunch and she's so forgetful once she gets engrossed in whatever she's doing–' She stopped and gazed around her. Quite reasonably, she had expected Mandy to be sitting in the sitting room but the sitting room was quite empty; except for

142

the small pair of white panties covered with pink hearts that lay accusingly in the middle of the carpet. We both stared at them. I heard Mrs. Thetiss swallow. She turned to me.

'Have you known my daughter long, Mr ... Mr ...' She frowned. 'I'm terribly sorry but I seem to have forgotten your name.'

'Paul. Paul Morgan.'

'Paul ... Mr Morgan?' She turned and looked at the panties again.

'Would you like a glass of wine, perhaps? It's just after twelve,' I said a little desperately.

'No, thank you,' she said in a prim voice.

'Oh, there they are! Hello mummy,' said Mandy, appearing fully dressed from the bedroom. She picked up her panties and twirled them around on her forefinger.

'Mandy!' said Mrs Thetiss before she could stop herself. 'Why aren't you wearing your pants?'

At that point the front door burst open to reveal Charles, larger than ever, dressed in a voluminous multicoloured kaftan and followed by one of the most beautiful young men I've ever seen in my life.

'Dear boy! Dear boy!' said Charles. 'Be still my beating heart! Half-naked as usual. He was half naked the last time I saw him, and that was twenty years ago!'

He enfolded me in the kaftan, hugged me tightly. 'Light of my life, how are you?'

'Well, Charles, very well.'

'Good. And the beard? That's new. You look deliciously classical. Praxiteles would be wild to sculpt you. But what happened to your nose?' Before I could answer, he turned dramatically and put an arm around his young companion who smiled charmingly at us. 'Paul, this is Damian. He's divinely talented,' he confided in a stage whisper.

'Hello, Damian.' We shook hands. 'Charles, Damian, let me introduce you to Mrs Barbara Thetiss and her daughter Mandy.'

I saw Charles's beady eyes light delightedly on the panties in Mandy's hand. Everyone said how do you do, and Charles asked Barbara the origin of her name. In the polite ensuing chatter I managed to pour white wine for Charles and Damian and a gin and tonic for Barbara. Mandy disappeared to my bedroom and when she returned her panties were no longer in evidence. She and her mother held a brief but intense private conversation under the pretext of dealing with the problem of the errant father's claim on Mandy's time, asked to use my telephone and after a few minutes returned to the porch where we were sitting in the pleasant spring sunshine.

Damian had taken off his shirt to catch the sun and I knew he was proud of his finely delineated muscles. I saw Barbara's eyes flicker quickly over his torso in the unobtrusive all-encompassing glance married women learn so quickly.

'I don't have to go to daddy any more,' said Mandy, kicking my ankle under the table while looking at Damian's chest with great interest.

'Then you must both stay to lunch,' I said firmly.

'But we couldn't possibly,' protested Barbara.

'Of course we can, mummy,' said Mandy, pleading. 'Paul's made huge amounts of food, and I helped him, and you've never seen so many crayfish. Please?'

'Don't be ridiculous,' said Charles. 'Of course you must stay. The child has shared in the labour and you are much too beautiful to refuse. Think how your presence will enhance our drab lives.'

She smiled at him and chuckled. 'Very well,' she said. 'Since you insist, we'd love to stay.' It's sometimes difficult not to smile at Charles.

When they were all chatting happily I excused myself and went into the bedroom to change into an old pair of jeans and a polo shirt. Mandy skipped into the room.

'Paul, thank you for asking us to lunch.'

'Mandy, get out of the bedroom. For God's sake! Your mother ... Think, Mandy!'

'Oh, don't worry about Mummy. She thinks I've come to get some wine. But please, please tell me that you know I love you and always will, no matter what happens.'

'Yes,' I said impatiently. 'I do.'

'Cross your heart?'

'Cross my heart. Now go.' She skipped back outside.

We ate lunch on the porch since the wind had dropped and the unexpected burst of spring sunshine had driven away the cloud. I sat next to Barbara, who was really very lovely. Her hair was the same pale toffee as Mandy's but brightened by streaks of sunbleach that only come from seawater and sunlight. She had very competent hands that I liked to watch.

The bouillebaisse had turned out well and everyone praised Mandy's rouille, which was stiff with garlic and chilli. I was pleased to see that Barbara enjoyed her food. She had none of the diet-driven pernicketiness of the vain. We chatted. It seemed she loved swimming, but had never dived. She seemed interested in my past.

'How do you know Charles?' she asked, spreading rouille thickly on a piece of toast.

'He lectured me at university,' I said, pouring her more wine.

'What did you read?'

'English and history. Charles was my drama lecturer.' She nodded. She was evidently not certain about my sexual proclivities.

'Did you enjoy university?'

'Very much.' I decided to put her out of her misery. 'I met my wife there.'

'You're married?' she said in surprise. 'From what Mandy told me I gathered you were a bachelor. A rather intriguing bachelor, actually, judging from the stories Mandy told me last night about some of your adventures in Africa. How did you break your nose?'

'It's not broken, it just looks like a potato. And I'm divorced.'

'And Charles?' she asked with a tiny smile.

'No.'

'He's rather nice, isn't he?'

'I adore Charles.'

'What does he do now?'

I explained that he was professor of drama at one of the smaller universities.

'He is very theatrical,' she said.

'Yes, he likes the Jacobean tragedies best of all. So do I. Very decadent and intense. What's funny though, is that he knows all the Elizabethan and Jacobean plays so well he often just bursts into blank verse. Very disconcerting until you get used to it.'

'I can imagine!'

Mandy was chatting animatedly to Charles and Damian. She was telling them about the sea, how she could tell its moods from the way it looks, what crabs eat, why Red Stumpnose have such bulbous heads and how to spot dolphins at a distance. Damian was interested but Charles, who hates beaches because of all the sand, was looking a little bored. Barbara noticed too and asked Charles a long question about Bacon and Shakespeare which he set about answering in great detail, commencing with a learned cryptogrammatical gloss on the word 'honorificabilitudinitatibus'.

Mandy and Damian were talking about rock music. I felt very old, listening to them, and found myself just a little envious of Damian. He looked so new-minted, so crisp-edged and precise whereas I felt blurred inside my skin. He had none of the shop-soiled look I saw every morning in my shaving mirror. Damian touched Mandy's hand briefly to emphasize some point and a feeling passed through me that I'd inadvertently set in motion a play I could no longer stop. Mandy was nodding at Damian and smiling. I watched as she cracked a crayfish claw between her teeth, a small anthropophagous smile on her face, and saw Eva as she must have looked when she was a teenager: self-contained, self-possessed, quietly predatory, waiting. Damian suspected nothing, poor boy.

The lunch was pronounced Jacobean in its decadence by Charles who loudly demanded 'sweetmeats' but fell asleep before I could give him coffee and pudding, his spectacles askew and his hands folded about the stem of his wineglass which rested comfortably on his paunch. The sun struck pale highlights from the choppy sea. The clouds were coming back stealthily, like stalking cats. I poured coffee, and Damian and Mandy consumed vast quantities of chocolate mousse. I decided to clear some of the litter from the table. Mandy and Barbara offerred to help but I poured them more wine instead and asked them to be good guests and enjoy the sun.

Damian followed me into the kitchen, carefully carrying plates.

'What an utterly divine lunch,' he said. I sensed he wanted an intimate little chat.

'Thanks Damian. Seafood always looks so good, doesn't it? That helps.'

'But your cooking! It was stunning.'

'Do you cook?' I asked, watching him as he stacked plates in the dishwasher.

'Someone has to. Charles is hopeless, can't even boil an egg.'

'You're living together, then?'

'Oh, good God, no! No, not at all! We share a house, that's all. No, I'm not gay, if that's what you think.' He shuddered elegantly at the thought and emptied mussel shells into the dustbin. 'I was first team rugby captain last year,' he added helpfully.

'Well, that must convince me,' I said sweetly, remembering that Charles once told me all his most passionate lovers came from the Stellenbosch rugby fraternity. 'And you're studying drama?'

'Yes. Under Charles.'

I let that pass.

'Mrs Thetiss's damn attractive, isn't she,' he said with a lewd little wink and a studied man-to-man smile. 'And the daughter. Naughty little thing. She reminds me of my first girlfriend in form one.'

'Yes. It's all that blond hair. She hardly looks thirty four.'

'Thirty four? Ready for a toy boy, I reckon,' he said. 'And Mandy's pretty hot, too.'

'You think so?' I said primly.

'Oh, yes. Shall I put these crayfish shells in the bin?'

'Please. What makes you so sure she's so hot, as you put it?'

'Oh, I had a little girlfriend of twelve last year. Crazy about me. You'd think she was deranged she wanted me so much.'

Charles had chosen an odd one this time. I confess I was a little confused.

'You've known Charles for absolute ages, haven't you,' he asked.

'Ages. He lectured me at varsity too.'

'He's good, isn't he? Brilliant?'

'Yes. He can turn out real actors rather than Eistedfodd winners, which is pretty remarkable. Most drama departments can't, because their lecturers have never actually worked in theatre.'

'Is that so? I'm delighted you say that, because I want to act more than anything.'

'It's not easy.'

'Why?'

'It's that transition from juvenile lead to leading actor to character actor. It's hard for the actors to accept; the inevitability of ageing. It won't be your problem for some time, though, will it?'

He shook his head and smiled at me, confident he'd never grow old, confident that he was barely mortal. Then he frowned. He looked like a puzzled angel. I sensed a major question.

'Paul, what should I do if Charles makes a pass at me?'

'He won't,' I said. I knew Charles too well.

'Why not?'

'Because he's a very ... moral person. What usually happens is that young actors try to seduce him, expecting him to advance their careers.'

He looked appalled. I watched and waited. He stacked plates expertly in the dishwasher, added detergent, closed the door with a thud. He must have been such a help to his mummy around the kitchen. Finally he said, 'It's just that for my career – I thought – it's the most important thing in my life ... the only thing, actually. So I thought, if I did, you know–well, if I didn't I thought he might not, if you see what I mean. You know, what you said.' He made an ineffectual gesture with his hand. It was a fine-boned hand and I suspected that much of his life would be taken up with ineffectual gesturing.

'Charles won't ruin your career if you don't sleep with him,' I said.

'And if I did?'

'Did you?'

He looked uncomfortable. 'No. But what if I did?'

'It's not going to get you anywhere, Damian,' I said. 'Charles's not like that. He's too concerned with his craft to be distracted by a pretty bottom.' He looked, I thought, very disappointed.

'And you? Were you?'

I was beginning to tire of his questions. 'Was I what, Damian?'

'Lovers. You and Charles?'

'No, Damian, I'm not gay.' He had the grace to look embarrassed and I took pity on him. 'Damian, let me tell you a story. When I was at university, Charles and I became friends. He taught me an awful lot. We shared interests in music and obscure Jacobean playwrights. And one night after we'd had a very good dinner at a restaurant that no longer exists, he said to me quite suddenly over the cognac, "Tell me, dear boy, are you gay?" "No," I said. "Oh, jolly good," he said with infinite relief, "Then we can be friends. Friendship lasts so much longer." And I agree with him. Do you understand?'

Damian nodded but looked even unhappier. Mandy walked into the kitchen carrying plates. 'You've been in here for ages,' she said.

'What've you been talking about all this time?' She glanced at Damian who still looked very troubled. She put the plates into the sink and turned to him briskly and punched him hard on the arm. He recoiled.

'That hurt!' he said. 'You little bitch!'

She laughed at him. 'I bet you've never seen a seahorse,' she said. 'Have you?'

'No, never,' he replied sullenly.

'Well, I know just where one lives,' she said.

'I thought they were fantasy creatures,' said Damian, rubbing his arm. 'You hurt me.'

'Don't be such a ninny,' she said scathingly, and turned to me.

'Mummy says if you touch a seahorse you'll never grow old.'

'Like Peter Pan?' said Damian. 'Really? Do you believe that?'

She grinned at him. 'Question is, do you?' she said. 'Do you?'

'I'd like to see one,' he said.

'Come on, then,' she said. 'I'll take you.' She opened the kitchen door and dragged him out into the thin sun. He went reluctantly. Mandy caught my eye.

'Do you remember what I said in the bedroom?' she asked very softly.

'Yes. Why?'

'Promise me you'll always remember it.' I hesitated.

'Promise me!'

'I can't promise that,' I said. 'Who could?'

'I could,' she said simply, but I didn't believe her. She ran forward and kissed me once hard on the mouth then turned away and took Damian's hand and dragged him off towards the beach.

'Don't be late,' I called. 'And watch the tide ... ' From behind the horizon there came the faintest drumming of thunder, a noise that Lockhart had once described to me as "a diabolus dancing on your coffin lid".

'And mind the storm,' I shouted, but they'd gone. I peered after them. They were walking off together, talking animatedly. I wondered why I felt such unease. Or was it simple jealousy?

THREE

Barbara Thetiss was smiling to herself and twirling the wine in her glass when I sat beside her at the table. Charles snored quietly but happily.

'I like your friend Charles,' she said softly. 'He's a lovely man.'

'Yes, Charles is very special. Would you like some port? And there's Stilton? Or Brie?'

'Good heavens, no. But I'd like a little more of that white, if it's still cold?'

'Of course.'

She sipped and sighed. 'Such a lovely wine. What year is it?'

'I've no idea. Not old. Whites don't last well, do they?'

'I know nothing about wine,' she said.

Silence fell. I watched a large black-backed kelp gull deftly pecking the eyes out of a dead fish that lay above the highwater line.

'Have you met that blind chap who lives down the bay?' she asked.

'Daniel Lockhart? Yes.'

'Does he have rather awful scar tissue on his forehead?'

'Yes. I've often wanted to ask him, but never had the courage. You know him?'

'Ages ago! Simply ages ago. I was in his first confirmation class, ages ago. We called him Father Dan. He was unfrocked.'

'What? Lockhart? A priest? Why?'

'Didn't you know?'

'Not at all. Why? You mean he was a priest but he's not any more?'

151

She shook her head. 'Not any more. And you don't know how he became blind?'

'No. How?'

'He shot himself,' she said softly. 'He tried to commit suicide and bungled it somehow. I gather he used some silly little gun, and muffed it. And the Jesuits took a jolly dim view of that, I can tell you! They chucked him out. I thought you probably knew.'

'No ... Why did he do it?'

She shook her head. 'No one knows. One day he just didn't come to class, a rather nasty priest with a face like a rat came instead, all ... smarm. Awful man. We only heard about it all much later. I always thought he'd lost his faith, but no one ever knew for sure.'

We sat in silence. I thought about Lockhart. Why hadn't he told me? Why hadn't he told me! Why had he shot himself? Silly man. He should have told me. Perhaps I could have helped him, the blind leading the blind.

I felt Barbara watching me. She spoke a little hesitantly. 'Paul, I must apologise; when I first saw Mandy's panties on the floor I thought ... I mean, you must think me awful. But, you see she's becoming a woman, and it's sometimes a little disconcerting to see one's daughter using ... feminine wiles on older men when she's only a teenager, a child still.'

I nodded. 'It must be.'

'She once had a brief flirtation with another much older man and told me everything.'

'Oh yes?'

'Yes. But still, to see her playing with fire the way she does ... ' she shook her head. 'It frightens me.'

'It must do. I had a stepdaughter. She was twelve when her mother and I were divorced. I saw the same thing. You can't stop the girls, they seem to flirt instinctively when they grow up. Like Mandy. She gave me grey hairs.'

'Mandy?'

'No, my daughter.'

'It seems such a pity.'

'Why?'

'They seem so perfect as children,' she said wistfully. 'It seems such a waste that all that perfection should be ditched as a sort of side-effect of growing up. It's rather like – did you ever suffer from acne as a teenager?'

'No.'

'I had a friend, such a lovely girl, so pretty, who suddenly burst out all over at fifteen with the hugest pimples. Her perfect prettiness was gone, almost overnight. All because of growing up.' She laughed wryly. 'It hardly seems worth it, does it?'

'We can't stop it, and it never stops, ever,' I said gently.

'What?'

'Growing up. It's always hard.'

'I suppose so,' she said slowly. I poured her a little more wine.

'Where did Mandy and Damian go?'

'To look at rock pools. To see a sea-horse. Eternal youth.'

'Ah; eternal youth,' she murmured.

'Peter Pan, Damian said. He looked delighted.'

She smiled. 'He would, wouldn't he! Those pretty boys!'

We sat in companionable silence and watched clouds forming over the sea. The intimacy made me uncomfortable.

'You're divorced, then?' she said suddenly.

'Twice,' I said without enthusiasm.

'Love wasn't lovelier the second time around?'

I didn't know how to answer that so I said nothing.

'Mine wasn't even lovely the first time around,' she confided.

'What happened?'

She hesitated. 'I don't actually know. He was a very jolly man. Always smiling. I was really rather impressed by him, he seemed so alive compared with the sort of men I'd grown up with. You know: swimming parties and tennis parties and matric dances and brother schools and sister schools and the sort of boys who are terribly good at cricket and rugby and smile a lot and seem to completely miss the point as they grow up.'

'I know what you mean.'

'They say thank you at all the right times and go off to university and do medicine or engineering or become lawyers and suddenly wake up when they're fortyish and discover they've learnt nothing at all and everything seems pointless to them. So they go off and find young women and leave their wives and behave like the little boys they still are.'

She looked at me. I nodded but thought it unwise to mention that everything seemed pointless to me too.

'But that wasn't what I wanted,' she said seriously, touching my arm. 'I'd seen those sort of men betray their wives so often, year after year, all my parents' friends were like that. I wasn't going to let it happen to me.'

'Very sensible.'

'Let me tell you a story. On my first day at university, I left and never went back. Do you know why?'

'I can't imagine. Your sociology lecturer had halitosis?'

She smiled slightly. 'No. I looked at all the intense little cerebral men around me, all utterly devoid of ... of true passion, and I was rather revolted. Then I saw some builders sitting on scaffolding high up in the air. They all had their shirts off in the hot sun and I liked them, not all the wimpish little men around me.'

I nodded obediently.

'And Taki – my husband – was a bit like that. He was Greek and he didn't go to university.'

'Neither did Shakespeare,' I said.

'Oh, he was no Shakespeare! He simply thought all that socially acceptable behaviour was stupid. He was a law unto himself. And he danced so well! I liked that. He seemed to be a sort of free spirit. Does that make sense?'

'Of course.'

'It took me ten years to discover that he wasn't really human, wasn't the way I'd imagined. He was just a facade and a small, nasty cruel little stunted thing inside that big man. He was nearly as big as you. Of course, we fought ... '

I listened to her catalogue the final events of their marriage: the suspicions and accusations and the cold rage and then the first fight and the shock of the pain felt and inflicted and her fear when she discovered the pitch of blind fury she could provoke in him. It was the inevitability of it all that bewidered her most; they seemed 'powerless to stop the rot.' It was as if another power had taken control, as if they were 'possessed'. They were no longer, she told me hesitantly, free to act.

'Why do we do it?' she asked. Not wanting an answer, merely wanting closeness.

'I don't any longer,' I said harshly, to put a stop to it.

'Youth, the illusions of youth, dear boy; you know that,' said Charles, yawning and stretching hugely. 'Is there any more wine?'

'How long have you been awake?' asked Barbara sharply.

'Seconds only. Thanks, that looks good,' he said as I filled his glass. He drank, straightened his spectacles, burped softly and said, 'Ageing is the process of losing one's illusions. Disillusionment shouldn't have the connotations it does. Disillusionment,' he intoned in his best lecturer's voice, 'is a Good Thing. It relieves us, eventually, of Hope; and Hope – as the poet noted – is often hope of the wrong thing. Without hope we cannot be disappointed. Without illusions, reality can never intrude rudely to awaken us. We are safe. Immune from folly, madness and strife, insulated from unhappiness. To live without illusion is to find true happiness.' He drank deeply again. 'Where is that slut Damian, by the way?'

'He went rock-pooling with Mandy,' answered Barbara.

'He did, did he?' murmured Charles.

Barbara frowned at him and I knew what she was thinking. I watched her. But for the little smile lines around her eyes she could have passed for her daughter's sister. Those long hours spent sweating in the gym had given her skin a sheen, her body a tautness that was strange in a woman. When she moved, muscles and tendons drew taut under her skin.

I felt a sudden urgent stirring as I looked at her, a nagging ache that reared up through me, deeper than the testes, surging from the prostate. I put my hand gently on her arm and saw the soft blond hairs rise under my touch. She turned with a start and stared back into my eyes and I knew that I was watching the same feeling loosen her, soften her.

Her lips opened as if to speak but she said nothing.

'Don't look at each other like that, it's indecent,' said Charles quietly. 'Particularly just after lunch.' He watched us, smiling gently. 'How long have you known this beast that wants discourse of reason?'

'What? Oh,' said Barbara. She took a deep breath. 'Just a few hours really. We met this morning. It feels longer, though. As though we've known each other for ages. I came to find my daughter.'

'After your daughter too, was he?' said Charles, maddeningly. 'Dear God, can nothing drain the cisterns of his lust?' Stupid bastard, I thought, drunk. But Barbara just laughed.

'I think I'll go and find Mandy,' she said. 'And Damian. We ought to be going. It's getting rather late.'

'It's not late yet,' I protested. 'The sun's still high.'

'But it goes down so quickly at this time of year. Dark before you know it,' she said. 'And it's nice to walk home along the beach.' She looked at me and I knew that she wanted me to walk along the beach with her. I said nothing.

'You're not worried about Damian, are you?' asked Charles. 'With Mandy? There's no need. He's not like Paul, Mandy's quite safe.' Barbara smiled at him, frowned at me and set off down the beach, trim, healthy, vibrant, but walking just a little more urgently than was necessary. She was obviously accustomed to getting her own way.

'How about some music?' said Charles.

'Of course. What?'

'None of those dreadful Beethoven string quartets you were so fond of, definitely not that awful Grosse Fugue you used to play; the one that sounded like someone having their head sawn off. And nothing obscure. I'd have to guess and that gives me indigestion. You choose.'

I put on a tape of the French Suites. Precise and intense, I knew they'd please Charles. The opening notes reminded me of the first time I'd heard them when I was in my freshman year at university.

'That's perfect,' said Charles.

'Do you remember playing this for me?'

'No. Did I? When?'

'In that rehearsal room at Hiddingh Hall.'

'Squalid place. Was there a piano?'

'Yes.'

'Funny, I do remember. I think I remember.'

'The music was beautiful.'

'Was it? Was I inspired and wonderful? Tell me I was.'

'As I remember it.'

'You sound very wistful. You're not falling in love again are you?'

'No. Never.'

'Never?'

156

'Never,' I said firmly.

Charles laughed. 'Never's an awfully long time.'

'And I mean it.'

'Ah. You've just got divorced again, haven't you. I heard about it. Was it awful?'

'Yes.'

'Very?'

'Yes.'

'Do you want to talk about it?'

'No.'

'Not yet?'

'Not ever.'

'What happened?'

'Oh, the usual,' I said, and I tried to say it casually. 'Young man, middle aged woman, lust.'

'Lust?'

'Yes, lust. Eva'd gone to some ridiculous encounter group to sort out her life, our life, which had got rather complicated, and she met a young man who was suffering torments from doing his national service and being shouted at by people who evidently didn't love him as much as his mummy did. I gather they thought they'd help each other; whining in unison about how unfair life is, I suppose. And that was that.'

'Oh dear, you do sound bitter. Were you in the army?'

'You know I wasn't Charles, they wouldn't take me because of my knee. Don't be silly.'

'Bit harsh of you to talk so glibly about that young chap. Was he an ordinary soldier?'

'Parabat, she says. But then, she says anything.'

'Oh dear. I had a boyfriend in the Parabats. They went through hell in the Angolan war. He used to wake up in the middle of the night, crying. I used to hold him like a little baby. I must say, I think you're very harsh.'

I looked at him. I'd never suspected this sentimentality. 'He volunteered, Charles. He chose his own fate, like all of us.'

'I still think you're being very harsh.'

'Do you? I don't.'

'What was he like?'

I shrugged. 'Tough but sensitive; strong but gentle. Tarzan with a psycho degree, her favourite fantasy. She'll dump him when she's sucked him dry.'

'Unfortunate image. Are they in love?'

'Love? Love? She says he likes her.'

'And?'

'And she's writing a play.'

'Is she?' said Charles with interest. 'What about?'

'Ah. It's very moving. It's about a very handsome, very intelligent young man suffering from angst who meets a much older woman who's beautiful and blond and sensitive and intelligent and sexy and they fall in love and live happily ever after –'

'– don't be such a bitch! –'

'– or until her teeth fall out; which given the age difference will be quite soon.'

'Oh dear, I wish you weren't quite so bitter. And Barbara Thetiss? The beautiful Mrs Thetiss? What about her?'

'No. Not at all. I hardly know her.'

'That's never deterred you in the past! And the girl?'

'Don't be absurd Charles, she's much too young.'

'Oh dear. And you're sure about the mother?'

'Yes. I told you: I don't fall in love any more. Perhaps I'm growing up, at last. I seem to be seeing women as they are, at last, rather than the way I pretend they are.'

'So you're no longer anima-obsessed? It didn't look like that to me, the way you were looking at each other. Aflame with lust.'

'Oh, Lord, thou pluckest me out, burning ... At one time I thought it would be nice to have someone. But lust's not love.'

'Don't be silly. Lust's wonderful, you know that. And you're ridiculous when you sound wistful.'

'I did have a strange feeling, earlier, that she ... that we were very close,' I said quietly.

'Yes,' he said. 'I saw.'

'But we weren't really.'

'No, I know.'

'Oh? How?' I asked.

He shrugged. 'She's not bright enough. Too desperate, too silly. More wine?'

'Of course.' I fetched another bottle of the Graves and poured him a new glass.

'Perhaps you need a demi-urge, not a damsel in distress,' he said thoughtfully as he sipped. 'My God, that's good.'

'Demi-urges can be very wearing. I've just survived one.'

'You like that, though, don't you?'

'Not any more, I'm tired. And you? Are you in love again?'

'With Damian?'

'Who else?'

Charles did not immediately reply. Some of the more daring surfers had begun to ride the treacherous but exhilarating progressive break that came at high tide to my bay, and two of them had caught Charles's eye as they walked past in their tight swimming costumes, their boards balaced one-handed on their heads, wetsuits tucked under the other arm, enjoying the unexpected sun. One had long blond hair, tended as carefully as a courtesan's. They walked with casual assurance, their universe defined, predictable, clear-cut as a military instruction. No ambivalence there. They were in their very early twenties, young, confident, still hard. I thought of Eva and for a moment the sadness came back and caught me by surprise.

'These silly young men,' said Charles in faint exasperation. 'Why do they think a fancy hairstyle will distract one from their acne scars? And anyway, Damian's not his real name, you know that,' he added. 'His real name's Harold.'

'And are you in love with Harold?'

Charles sighed. 'No, no, no, no. But you must admit he's very beautiful.'

'Very.'

'He seduced me, you know,' he said, with the faintest hint of pride.

'He's beautiful to look at,' I said.

'That only?'

I shrugged.

'Nothing else?' he insisted.

'I don't know,' I said.

'Not only beautiful. But I don't know what's wrong with him. Every time we make love he tells me he's not gay.'

'Awful.'

'Yes. And there's this whole AIDS thing. Sex isn't the same for us.'

'Spare me the details.'

'I will, I will.' He drank some more wine.

'And Philip? What happened to Philip?' I asked.

'Monstrous child!'

'And Andre?'

'Don't be absurd. That was years ago. An illusion to be dispensed with.'

'Why do you look so done in then, if you've lost all your illusions and found happiness?'

He sighed and held out his glass for more wine. 'In the first place, I didn't say I had, I merely held that up as an ideal to strive for. And secondly, my life has become a most dreadful burden to me. It's partly my mother.'

'She must be quite old now ... '

'And very ill. The worst is, they can't seem to decide what's wrong with her.'

'Oh damn. I am sorry.'

'Cancer they say Monday, Tuesday it's a motor-neuron disease.'

'Oh, Damn! Jesus ... '

'She's turned to Him, of course.'

'Lockhart will be surprised.'

'Who's Lockhart?'

'My priest from down the bay.'

'Your priest? Your priest?'

'No. My neighbour. He's not really a priest.'

'And there's the business of ageing itself,' he went on.

'You haven't aged.'

'Come on! Of course I have. So have you. Look at that gut on you. I remember when you were a svelte young thing and every woman in town wanted to lay you, come on. Of course we've aged.' There was a pause.

'Have I offended you?' he asked softly.

'No, not at all. I was thinking about Wordsworth.'

'Not for this faint I nor mourn, nor murmur?'

'Precisely.' He smiled at me and I laughed. I'd chosen that passage for a crit class in my first year and had the woman adjudicator in tears with the intensity of my delivery and was terribly impressed by myself. I only discovered later that her tears were tears of mirth.

'But there's no abundant recompense,' I said. 'That I can see. Eliot was right. Remember the aged eagle.'

'Ah ... the gifts reserved for age to set a crown upon your lifetime's effort ... '

160

'... the cold friction of expiring sense blah blah.'

'Blah blah. Yes, but that's not your problem,' he said slyly. 'You don't suffer from expiring sense; if anything you're more sensual than ever. You want to taste it all, squeeze it dry. But you don't trust the sensation any more, do you? You've sucked the oysters down and now you're left with a dead feeling, emptiness, and your faith swore it wouldn't, couldn't, be like that. Am I right?'

I nodded.

'It's the knowledge of its terrible quick passing, Paul,' he said. 'Terribly hard. My thirties. I survived them, but there's less of me now. God knows what my forties will bring. Less of the same, I suppose.'

'You really shouldn't complain,' I said harshly. 'You sound as though you've given up. For no reason. You're not dead yet, nor ill, unlike your mother. All you need is someone close to you to die and you'll see things straight. And besides, you forget how that last bit goes, something about "... you must move in measure, like a dancer."'

Charles laughed long and loud at that, groaned, wiped tears of delight from his eyes, applauded, cheered, downed his wine and waved for more, drank that down and when his mirth had spent itself, gestured at his comfortable bulk in the kaftan. 'Can you imagine? Me? A dancer? Come on, dear boy, I'm too fat to be a dancer, even a metaphysical one. And what's more, so are you!'

I hadn't thought of that.

161

FOUR

As the soft yellow afternoon tumbled towards sundown everything fell apart quite suddenly. Our flimsy centre had not held, anarchy was loosed upon our little world.

Even when Charles and I saw them approaching from a distance along the beach we knew something had gone terribly wrong. The thunderbolt steers all, said wise Herakleitos with disarming simplicity. We watched the three figures walking towards us. For an instant I was convinced they were masked actors in an ancient drama, or the Eumenides sent to try us. But when they drew closer the illusion passed and they were merely people.

Barbara was distraught. She could hardly speak. Her eyes were red. Damian looked smug and stared arrogantly at Charles. Then I saw the look of pride and wonder on Mandy's face and knew exactly what had happened. Charles knew too; and despite his earlier denials I knew that Damian meant much more to him than he cared to admit. He would surely spend long nights pondering this latest revelation of the thunderbolt's deft plotting.

Barbara and Mandy disappeared inside. Damian followed to fetch his jersey. Charles and I stood alone outside. A single tern winged past and I watched it out of sight.

'Paul. I'm most awfully sorry about all this,' said Charles. 'I don't know what to say.'

'No matter. It's not your fault, don't be silly.'

'I'm sorry because of the woman. Do you think she would've made you happy?'

'No,' I said. 'No, I don't think so.'

'No, nor do I.'

'Besides, I'm not convinced that happiness is important for me.'

'No,' he said with a small smile. 'It's not your lot, is it.'

'Evidently not.'

Damian walked up. He'd knotted his jersey fetchingly around his neck. He held out his hand as if he were the Pope offering his ring to be kissed.

'Sorry about all the drama. No hard feelings?'

I shook my head. 'None!' We shook hands gravely, like two rugby captains.

'Goodbye,' said Charles.

'Goodbye.'

'Goodbye, Paul,' said Damian.

'Goodbye.'

'I'll phone you,' said Charles. 'Come on, Harold. It's time to go. And for God's sake don't flounce ... '

They turned and walked off down the beach. I paused to watch them. Despite Charles's rotundity and age, it struck me that he moved with a strange elegance; almost in step with the rhythm of the cosmos; almost, in fact, like a dancer.

I went inside, not certain what I'd find. Barbara was still in tears. Mandy was smiling. Barbara sent Mandy to fetch tissues from her car and turned to face me. Her nose was red where her makeup had rubbed away. Her mascara had run slightly. She ran a nervous hand through her thick hair and smiled a small sad smile.

'Paul, I know we only met this morning and I know you probably think this strange but quite frankly I simply don't know what to do, how to cope with Mandy's latest – escapade. You guessed what happened?'

I nodded. 'There's nothing you can do,' I said. 'It was bound to happen sooner or later.'

'Yes, but not like this!'

'How then?'

'I don't know – love perhaps? I don't know.'

'What if she can't make love to the person she truly loves?' I said.

'What? Whatever can you mean?' she snapped. 'That's ridiculous.'

'I expect so,' I said. How could I tell her that I felt betrayed too?

'And that wretched boy just laughed at me! He laughed at me ... Am I getting old? Do people happily behave like this today? What did I do wrong?' She broke off, shook her head. 'He laughed at me! And it's not just the humiliation; what if he's got AIDS? He's homosexual, after all.' She shook her head in confusion.

'Barbara, I'd like to help, but I've got no answers. I don't even know what questions to ask any more. I'm like you. I can't help.'

'Dear God, I wish Daddy was here, he'd know what to do,' she said with a malevolent little glance at me. 'He's a man, he'd know exactly what to do!' Perhaps she expected me to horsewhip Damian.

'Is that what you call him?' I asked quietly.

'Who?'

'Daddy.'

'Daddy? Of course I call him Daddy,' she said in a slightly shrill voice. 'Why not? Why shouldn't I call him Daddy, he's my father, I've always called him Daddy. You sound just like my mother! Why shouldn't I call him Daddy?'

'No reason,' I said.

Her mouth was set in a grim line. Then I saw her regain control and she smiled at me. 'I'm sorry,' she said. 'I just feel a bit shocked. And I thought, somehow, that you and I could be friends.'

I looked at her and hesitated before saying, 'Barbara, let's be honest: we could have been friends, even fallen in love briefly.'

She frowned. 'Why briefly?'

'Because we would've loved each other for things that weren't real. I think you see me as calm, serene, stoical, wronged, wounded, amusing, sexually adept. Unfortunately, all that's an illusion. I'm no mystical seer. What you take for serenity is resignation; what seems to you stoicism is actually hopelessness. My despair I cope with using ironical detachment, and that looks like wit. Wronged I'm not, wounded I am, but with just cause. And my sensuality is desperation. I've performed every sexual act so often with so many women that I'm desperate for my boredom to be lifted, and I wrongly assume that will happen if I perform the same acts with you.

164

Too much sex with the wrong people is like saying one word over and over again: eventually it becomes absurd.'

She stared at me in horror. 'How can you say all this? I know how you could be, how we could be together.'

I shook my head. 'No, Barbara. Last year perhaps, but not now. I'm finished.'

She stared at me earnestly, doubting her own intuition. 'But I thought . . .'

I nodded. 'Yes, I know you did, so did I. But we were both wrong.'

She stared, nodded, gave me a brisk, brave smile. 'Wrong again! You're right. I've learnt not to pretend that things are right when they're wrong.'

'You're right. We'd have been wrong.'

She picked up the framed photograph of my wife and the child.

'Is this your wife?'

'Yes.'

'She's very beautiful. They both are. Do I know her?'

'Perhaps. You're very alike, actually.'

'Perhaps that's why, earlier, I thought that you and I could be . . . .'

She replaced the photograph with an air of finality and called Mandy who appeared instantly, still smiling.

'Goodbye, Paul.' said Barbara.

'Goodbye. I'm glad we met.'

'Yes. So am I.'

'Goodbye Mandy. Please pop in any time you want to.'

'Goodbye. I'll come and visit you, and Ludwig.' She winked at me.

'Goodbye.'

'Goodbye.'

'Goodbye.'

I enjoyed a gloriously indulgent moment of self-pity and self righteousness as I watched them walk off down the beach together as stiff as strangers, Barbara and her pretty bloody daughter, both of them so long-legged and lithe; and for an instant I wondered whether growing up had been worth it after all.

I watched them until they grew small against the vastness of beach and sky and ocean, and then turned back, blinded by the sunset light, to look at the sea. The big black-backed gull I'd noticed earlier had pecked the eyes from the fish it was eating and now began to disembowel it, pulling at a long pallid strand of flesh, legs braced. Two other gulls stood nearby, watching beadily. Out beyond the breakline a flock of gannets hovered, plummeted on neatly folded wings and hit the sea in white splashes, divebombing a sardine shoal. The light was a thick and luminous citron. A sour lemon-segment of moon showed against the creeping dark.

Watching this, I thought: here I am at the midpoint of my life, the still centre of my turning world and I have learnt nothing, absolutely nothing. I have come to this point without profit to my spirit, loveless and unloved, all with good reason. All my expectations of joy were misplaced, the long-awaited harmony and wisdom all fictions, the coming humiliations more subtle and far less dramatic than I could ever have foreseen.

· And I have no child to bear my genes into the future, no child to love selflessly without expectation of love in return, no child with whom to share simple delights, no child to carry my memory for a short generation while my own body grows cold in its undertaker's cloths. Stupid, self-pitying, self deceiving even in this, I realized that I had always thought Eva and I would one day be together again, that this bleak time was a caesura only, a loveless interregnum, not a fact, unredeemable and inescapable.

But now I knew that it would not be so. She would pursue her life with her succession of young lovers and I would be always alone, growing more silent and fractious by the year. Even my quest for spirit was vain, empty, the vacuous posturing of a tired middle-aged man unable to commit himself to people, impatient for the end of deep affection, keen to douse the stubborn fire of the heart's dour flamekeepers. I could sense that my connection with the universe had rotted away like a septic umbilical cord over the years. The sustaining bloodflow of the sun and sea and wind and stars, of love given and received no longer pulsed into me. I was alone with the silence between the stars.

Standing there on the beach of that heaving ocean I waited in vain for the sea to work its healing magic, but this time nothing came. Voracious for salvation, I sensed the god abandon me. There was nothing dramatic about this. Years ago I had allowed Eva to plant some rotten seed in the foul womb of my soul and it had died and slowly corrupted my spirit. Now I was hollow.

As if in confirmation, the dolphins came to fetch me while I was standing there staring at the blinding sunset light, my eyes full, looking into the heart of light, hearing the endless silence. A black sickle-curved fin broke the quiet surface. As I watched another followed, and another. At first I thought they were sharks: I had seen sharks there often before and these fins were so black and curved so cruelly, like a predator's fang.

I watched them move in the clear water, watched their languid play as they surfed lazily down the face of each small wave that broke there, watched their dark shadows flicker across the rippled sand. In their swimming you could sense a pitch of joy, a rush of pleasure from their very quick. They loved their element so deeply and I wondered how it was that I had lost my innocence. When had I fallen? There was a simple answer to that: one hot yellow day in central Africa when I understood finally that Eva could never love me wholly, even if she wished to.

Kalilombe and I had marched into camp, each carrying one of the long sap-stained hundred pound tusks. The kitchen staff saw us first and ran out with loud cries of welcome and amazement, because in Africa these days tusks like that are a rarity and a wonder. Coletrane appeared too, a tight, contained smile on his face; and Eva, looking lovely and desirable in a cool white dress. There were two visitors in camp, old friends of Coletrane's; but Justin, the young hunter, was off on a shooting safari. Everyone clustered around to hear our story and when we had told it briefly the camp staff took charge of the ivory and carried it away with much oohing and aahing and Eva and I went to the chitenje where I was introduced to Coletrane's friends, whose names and faces I can no longer remember.

There, in the sticky heat, we had afternoon tea. The conversation flowed and ebbed around me but I was not listening because I could see in Eva's eyes that she had surrendered her body to Justin. And then it happened. Eva was sitting on a low canvas camp chair and Coletrane stood behind her, his hands resting paternally on her shoulders. There was a quiet inward smile on Eva's face, a smile I had never seen before, a smile of satisfaction and triumph. I immediately knew that I was about to witness something shameful, something that two people less convinced of the world's stupidity would've kept concealed. But they did not.

As I watched, his hands moved softly on her shoulders and then with a small, unobtrusive but somehow obscene little shuffle he moved his body closer to hers until his groin was pressed against the back of her neck. It was a small secretive movement, and I did not believe that I had seen it. I felt myself swallow and I looked around but no one else had noticed. Eva still had the same lost, sweet smile of complete satisfaction on her face and her father still smiled his affable smile while he chatted to his guests.

I felt hot, weak, out of touch and then I saw Eva's body thrusting up at Justin's, her eyes closed and turned up like a drunk's, tears squeezed out beneath her eyelids, rooting after orgasm like a pig after truffles while the dark stud above her loomed into her consciousness like a god, like her Daddy: the ridges of muscle in his abdomen coiling and rippling, his face a blank, buttocks clenched with effort. And at last I understood. I excused myself and walked away and vomited up tea and biscuits in a long hot stream behind the nearest tree.

It took me a year to come to terms with what I'd seen and one night when Eva was baiting and taunting me I broke my covenant with myself. It was one in the seemingly endless series of wild midnights that plagued us, internecine raids on each other's self-esteem and the frail parts of one another's psyches which we'd discovered over the years and kept secret as our hatred grew. Mercifully, the child always slept through these fights, despite the noise.

Finally, when I could endure her jeering no longer, I said, 'If I'm so bad, what about your precious daddy who pretends to be so holy?'

She stared at me in dismay. 'What? What do you mean? How dare you bring Daddy into this!'

'Yes, Daddy, pressing his cock into your back, you slut!'

'You bastard! You vile little bastard. How dare you say that about Daddy.'

'Ah. You deny it? You deny he did it?'

168

'Daddy would never do a thing like that. Never!' This came out in a long scream.

'Yes he did. I saw him. And I saw him do it to that silly old bitch Diana, too!'

'You didn't,' she shouted. 'He wouldn't. Never. Not ever. Not my Daddy. Never. Only with me, not with her, never with her! Daddy loves me, not her. I am Africa, Daddy loves Africa!'

I looked at her. Hair in maenad disarray, wild eyes that regarded me the way you look at a stone, or a layer of dust discovered under a newly lifted carpet. I wanted to say, Let's stop this, now; remember: when we make love I am the sea driving in at your mouth and you are my tides and moon-change, I am your full moon and diastole, but I said nothing.

'We're finished. Finished. How dare you, you bastard. Bastard bastard bastard. Ugly bastard. You've killed me. Do you hear me? You killed me! Jesus, if Daddy could hear what you've done to me he'd put a bullet through your brain. Bastard. Shitty little small minded bastard. You fake! Pig. Pig.' She paused for breath, panting, mouth slack and agape. After such knowledge, what forgiveness?

'Bullshit.' I said coldly. 'Bullshit. Whatever happened to you, you did yourself. Face it. Grow up.'

'You Judas!' she spat out.

'Judas? If I'm Judas, you're Jesus Christ, and even I don't believe that!'

Teeth gritted with fury she darted forward and grabbed a fistfull of my hair and shook my head wildly and shrieked, 'That's not true! And we're finished. Finished! See? Hear me? Finished finished finished finished you ugly bastard; I fucked Justin and I loved it! Hear me? I loved it. He came all over me, everywhere, places you haven't ever, again and again, and I loved it! Hear me? I loved it, I couldn't get enough!'

In a fury I turned away and found the .44 magnum beside the bed and slammed out of the room and went outside into the hot night, feeling the walnut grips smooth in my hands. The air was thick with jasmine.

'Yes! Yes!' she shouted from inside. 'Go on! Shoot yourself. Go on, you're too shit scared to. Make me happy! Shoot yourself.' I put the barrel of the revolver in my mouth.

'I fah-ucked Justin, I fah-ucked Justin, I fah-ucked Justin . . .'
she chanted in a jeering, sing-song schoolyard rhythm. I drew
back the hammer, heard two crisp clicks as the rebates
engaged the trigger sear. I could hear Eva screaming now, a
long incoherent wail of fury, curses and abuse. Or was she
simply crying all alone again?

I don't know if you've ever placed the barrel of a .44
magnum revolver in your mouth with the intention of killing
yourself. If you have, you will know that it is not dignified.
The high ramped front sight forces you to open your jaw
wide, and the metal of the barrel is cold on your tongue. This
is real. Pull the trigger now and the rest is silence. I stood
there in this stupid posture for a long time, my finger poised
on the trigger, listening to the calm night sounds: crickets
rasped, dogs barked, the darkness waited. I was not crying
but tears of self-pity ran down my face. I know: it was not real
and I should have realised that but I didn't. And this was
Eva's great skill: she bewitched you into inhabiting her
shadow land where you could not tell right from wrong, nor
distinguish the real from her tormented inner world.

Standing there, I became aware that a bar of light had fallen
across me. I turned and met the calm gaze of Eva's daughter,
staring at me between the opened curtains of her bedroom.
She watched me in silence for a long time as I stood there like
an idiot with the gun barrel in my mouth, her eyes quiet and
knowing. Then she turned away and closed her curtains again
and the light went out in her bedroom. Slowly reality came
back to me. She was right: it was up to me to choose. I carefully
withdrew the barrel from my mouth, lowered the hammer and
went back inside. Eva was lying on our bed, curled up around
her pillow, sucking her thumb like a baby. There was nothing
left to say. I locked the revolver away and went to sleep on the
couch in the sitting room. We never spoke to each other again.
Eva took her daughter and left the next day.

Now, looking at the dolphins, I knew that they had come to
fetch me. They wanted me to swim with them in their dark
sea. They were patient, but I could never again surrender; all
my love was gone. I turned away, walked back to the beach
house, unlocked the gun safe and took out the .44 magnum. At
that stage I did not know why. The metal was cold in my
hands. I went back to the rocks.

The dolphins were still there, waiting. I placed the barrel of the revolver in my mouth and drew back the hammer. This was absolutely real: no pretense was possible. Eternity was within my compass. I felt my finger tighten on the trigger. Then I smelt the acrid tang of gun oil in my sinus and for a second my mind was filled with a vision of hot dry grass, the smell of gun oil and sweat, of dust and heat, and I felt the dead weight of the rifle on my shoulder and saw Kalilombe turn to me and say: No map of Plain of Darkness; your map here. And he tapped my forehead at the exact point where the two hundred and fifty grain bullet would exit my skull if I pulled the trigger.

The sea paused between two waves and I heard a gull call, shrill and flinty. It was a clear, living sound and, startled, I withdrew the barrel from my mouth, lowered the hammer, weighed the revolver for a second in my hand and then hurled it as far out to sea as I was able. It tumbled end over end, glinting, then disappeared with a small splash just beyond the breakline. When I looked, the dolphins had gone.

I walked back to the house. Someone in one of the cottages along the seafront was playing a recording of the Laudate Dominum from Mozart's Solemn Vespers, but hearing it I felt nothing, absolutely nothing, and that fact made me laugh.

★

Back at the beach house I poured a double gin and tonic and pulled on a jersey and went out onto the porch to watch the sea. The storm was knotting clouds on the horizon. Out there the sea was as jagged as sharks' teeth. I settled comfortably in my camp chair and sipped my drink. The bruised lemon was tart on my tongue and palate. I wanted to keep this feeling of clarity, of invulnerability but I knew it would not be easy. I would have to find a way to keep it close to me forever. I thought of Lockhart: perhaps now I had found this still centre in myself I would be able to help him.

The dark clouds had prowled closer. Driven by the lurking storm the cormorants were hurrying back to their roosts on Cannon Rock. I watched them circle once and glide in to land, legs extended, pinions beating. They stood with black wings spread against the wind. I realised that I had forgotten Ludwig. The small dramas of lunchtime and after had made

171

me forget the truly important matter at hand, and as the sun finally settled below the horizon I went to give him his tablets and a hug, but I was too late.

He was lying there in his basket, too sprawled for life, his forepaws neatly crossed, tongue showing pinkly between his clenched teeth, lips pulled back in a small rictus, quite dead. There was a minute bead of blood on his tongue where his teeth had pierced the flesh. His silver muzzle was still warm. I sat on the floor and held him and felt the warmth of his body drain slowly out against mine until he became stiff. When I felt sure that his soul had finally left his body I wrapped him in his favourite blanket and carried him outside. The evening had turned chill. The stars were cold, their light as crystalline as seasalt. How could I have forgotten him? How could I have allowed him to die alone? I had been too self-absorbed to hear, too vain to know. Some sins stay with us even when our own bones are light and dry; when our own ligaments have rotted through they will still cling to us, never released. This I must learn to live with.

I buried him in amongst the sand dunes where he loved to run, the wind in his ears, stupid bastard, chasing seagulls. As an afterthought, I placed on top of his body the Tuareg cross that Diana Cheveley had given me. Perhaps it would help him. But I spoke no silly words; and worst of all, no tears came, even when I thought they should. Asleep forever beneath the shifting sands would he ever, I wondered, dream of me as I would dream of him?

That evening, alone in my armchair with a double tot of Laphroaig for company and 'The Cloud of Unknowing' lying unread in my hand, my dark spirit full of the sad adagios of night, my ears full of the storm's dull thunder, I thought of the wife who had left me, the child who would grow old without me. And when I heard the tap-step of Lockhart come up the path in the rain, I listened to his knock but could not open to him even though I wanted to; listened to his tap-step slowly leave again.

Late that night when the Pleiades had sunk and the sky was black and waiting for dawn I went to bed and found under my pillow Mandy's six salacious polaroids and her pair of white panties covered with pink hearts. The little bitch.

EPILOGUE

Now you see
The strength of love I bear to you
When I forget our vanity, and go
Treating our shadows like solid things.

Dante: The Divine Comedy: Purgatory:
Canto XXI

All this happened a long time ago, when it seemed I was still young. Now more than half my life is behind me and I have begun to hear the faint but insistent whispers of mortality.

Last year for the first time I went back to the plot where the beach house had stood. I'd never sold the land and often thought of rebuilding the house there after it collapsed, worm-gnawed, that winter long ago, but somehow my heart was never in it.

But last year when I finally descended the familiar concrete steps and heard the thumping swells break on Cannon Rock and saw the small slack-tide waves run swiftly up the rough winter shingle, and tiny sandpipers twinkling on quick feet along the tideline, I found to my surprise that I had come home at last and the place now held no terrors for me. A group of young surfers and their girlfriends stood on the beach, watching the waves.

I walked to the plot. Over the years, long grass had grown up through the bleached beams and grey rain-warped roof tiles. Tramps and beach bums had built fragile shelters from the joists and rotten ceiling boards, and used some of the timber for fires. But the foundations were still solid and I could see where the kitchen had been, and the bedroom, remembered how we had held each other tight in the winter chill. Gulls overhead cruised closer and began to scream at me.

Full of memories I walked down to the beach and trudged along the high-water mark. A crowd of delicate grey and white gulls flew off ahead of me, scavenging the tideline, chased by a black labrador puppy. The surfers were all talking excitedly, pointing out to sea. I stopped and shaded my eyes to look but could see nothing. I walked up to them and asked what they were looking at. They turned and stared at me, two young men, two girls, with the indifference that youth often displays to age.

'The whale,' said the tall blond boy abruptly.

'Winnie the Whale,' added one of the girls. Sixteen? Seventeen? She had a pretty smile, sea-tangled blond hair and candid eyes. I looked out to sea. At first I could see nothing, but then the whale's huge slow caudal fin broke the surface in a white burst of sunlit spray and disappeared gradually again beneath the water.

'See? She's calving in the bay,' said the young girl. 'Isn't that great?'

'Shit, check that, her tail's covered in barnacles, did you see that?' said the other boy excitedly.

'Calving?' I said in wonder.

'Yes. Every year for years. It's great to see,' said the blonde girl.

'Yes, it is,' I said, watching the sea.

'Hey, dint you used to live here?' asked the tall surfer. 'In that house that burnt down?'

'Yes,' I said slowly. 'But that was a long time ago.'

'Sure, before we discovered this terrific progressive left hand break here. I remember. I was really small, just a kid.'

'You're still just a kid,' said the blonde girl wryly. She turned to me. 'All the kids used to say you were a witch,' she said and giggled. 'Are you?'

'A warlock,' corrected the dark girl who hadn't spoken till now.

'Okay, warlock.'

'Or a priest,' added the tall surfer. 'They said your house was full of skulls and stuff.'

'It was,' I said. 'But I think you're confusing me with someone else. I'm not a priest, nor a warlock, nor a witch.'

'What are you then?' asked the dark girl.

'No man in particular,' I said. This seemed to satisfy them and they transferred their attention to the whale.

'You say the whale comes here every year to give birth?'

'Every year,' said the blond girl firmly. The black labrador puppy ran up and danced around my legs. I knelt to pat him. His pink tongue lolled happily.

'Is this your puppy?' I asked. They all shook their heads.

'He's always on the beach,' said the dark girl. 'We don't know who he belongs to.'

I decided in that instant to rebuild my house. But this time I would not use wood; this time I would build my house with stone quarried from rocks standing hard by the edge of the dolphins' sea.

It is not the same as before, how could it be? Everything, all of us, suffered a sea-change in the intervening years. It is not the same, but it will do. I moved in six months ago. The surfers and their girlfriends have become good friends and sometimes come to visit me to alleviate what they no doubt see as my corrosive loneliness but I haven't the heart to disillusion them. The labrador favours me with visits too, and often walks with me along the beach, chasing seagulls and trotting happily in the shallows.

Lockhart is gone, no one knows how; although there is a rumour that he was swept off the rocks by a freak wave while fishing. I am not convinced. I suspect the dolphins claimed him. Someone has erected a small granite cross on the rock that was his favoured fishing spot. Each month, winter and summer, a dark blue Bentley draws up quietly in the parking lot above the beach and a well-wrapped figure emerges and descends the path and stands for an hour beside the cross, facing out to sea. I have never approached her, but I sometimes stand where she stood and think about Lockhart and wonder.

The dark corrugated iron church at Bakoven is still there, and on my bad days I walk along the beach to light a candle for all the people I love who have gone, but without much faith. The wreck where we dived is more rusted, the superstructure beaten down by the untamed winter seas, and when the winds drive the savage unbroken swells in on the weather side, a plume of spray still issues high and white from the broken funnel and falls back into the sea like rain.

One day a tall blond woman knocked at my front door and I immediately recognised the Curacao-blue eyes and the toffee-coloured hair, still wild, and the naughty eyes. She was a child no longer and I felt myself approve of the woman she'd become. Her body had changed – chunkier through the hips, face weathered a little by sun – but the sulky beauty was still intact, her legs still elegant and finely muscled. It was wonderful to see her. She stayed for an hour and we chatted as easily as before and drank gin and laughed at the past.

She married young – no surprise to me – a man much older than herself. The marriage ended in divorce. She later married a beautiful Mauritian boy. When she showed me the pictures in her wallet she smiled with fine irony. He was dark, pliant, androgynous. That marriage lasted two years. She now lives at Llandudno, further down the coast, with her lover of five years, a wry dark woman of forty with hair cropped short like a boy's. Mandy works at the Oceanographic Institute on the Dolphin Research Project. She told me the dolphins have never returned to my small bay, and on summer field trips she is forced to travel far up the east coast to find them. When she left that day we promised to keep contact, but I have not seen her since.

I found Ludwig's grave amongst the shallow dunes. The winds had shifted some of the dunes, bulldozed new, flattened others. It was strange to think of all that vitality and vibrant flesh gone to a heap of ant-scoured bones, lying neat and bleached beneath the sand, the silver Tuareg cross resting forever over his untenanted heart.

I sat there for a long time in the wind and thought of him, thought of my grandparents, and my mother and father; thought of Eva and her child, all lost and gone for ever from my life. Eva: swimming deep in the pool of her new lover's breathing, would she ever remember me?

Thinking this, I recalled the bronze copy of Shiva's cosmic dance of creation that Lockhart gave me when I left the beach and tried fruitlessly to make a life elsewhere. I reminded myself that the god bore the fire of destruction on high; remembered too the meaning of the position of the right hand: 'Do not be afraid.' I have it still. It provides me with new conundrums every day, and insights I doubt I will have the time to use.

Often when I walk the beach I have the same feeling of immanent presences that I felt when my wife and child and I lived in our terra-cotta house built on the old graveyard at the foot of the cobbled streets of the Bo-Kaap. Perhaps these restless phantoms are remnants of all the seamen who died over the centuries in the seas hereabouts, or traces of the faded but undying fire that drove all the people I love during their lives in this time of despair.

I am unsure. I have not learnt yet how to tongue my mortal speech with fire so it will echo in the ears of the dead, so the unquiet ghosts remain silent, their mute questions forever unanswered. Perhaps all will come with time; although I have little enough of that left.

As I said, though the new house is built on the same ground as the old, it is not the same house. How could it be?

But the sea is still the same. Still relentless, still full of many gods, great mystery and many voices; just as it was when I lay waking beside my sleeping wife and listened to her breathing and watched her face pale and lovely in the light of the storm moon; lying close beside her in our wooden house at the edge of the waiting sea.